Cash Captured My Heart 3

Saved by a Boss

The Finale

By. Tyanna and Jammie Jaye

Cash Captured My Heart 3

Copyright © 2020 by Tyanna & Jammie Jaye

Published by Tyanna Presents

www.tyannapresents1@gmail.com

Synopsis

Things are starting to get heated when greed takes over. Meia wanted Luke, but the feelings weren't mutual. So, she tried to move on. What happens when her night and shining armor ends up changing her life for the worst? Luke and Shawnee were doing great until Meia comes along with her drama causing a minor setback in their happy home. Will Shawnee and Luke make it, or will Luke push her away because of everything that's going on.

Cash's record wasn't squeaky clean just yet. He still had one big hidden secret that was bound to mess up his future. Will Kyndall stick by his side or will she go on one of her disappearing acts? Will their love for each other be enough? Find out in the finale of *Cash Captured My Heart*!

Meia

"Tory, you are fucking me too hard!" I yelled. He had been taking lines back to back all day, and that shit was killing me. He was mad at Keys because he wouldn't let him borrow money. He had changed the most in two weeks. Like, this nigga was a whole new person. Just a week ago, he treated me like a queen; now he had me out here selling my pussy like I was a two-dollar hoe.

"Shut up before you fuck up my nut," he yelled back while yanking my hair. I knew he had to have a handful of my hair when he stopped.

I was so happy when he nutted. I grabbed my shit and went out the door. I was dry, so there was no reason to wipe myself off, and my shit burned like a motherfucker. It felt like someone had stuck a firecracker in my pussy, or like I had sniffed a line with my pussy. Y'all know what I mean. Hell, that shit hurt.

"Don't come back without my bait, either!" he yelled as I ran out the door. Everything in me wanted to say fuck it and never come back here, but I knew he would find me, just like I knew Luke would. I was so fed up and frustrated.

I jumped in my car and headed to my house. I hadn't been there in a while because I didn't want Tory to know I still had it. Hell, he would try and sell the motherfucker just to get high. I was fucked up, but not like him. Once I made it home, I headed to the shower. I needed to think of a way to get Joi. I wouldn't let Tory hurt her; I just wanted to get some money out of Luke.

The whole time I was in the shower, I was trying to think of a way to get her. I had tried the thing with his mom, but she wasn't going for it. She told me she couldn't go behind Luke's back like that. Joi wasn't in school, and I knew he wouldn't just let me come get her.

"Fuck, how can I pull this off?" I yelled. After I got out the shower, I called my mom to see if she would get her.

"Mom, I wanna see my baby," I fake cried.

"Don't call me with that bullshit. The last time I helped you, Luke wouldn't let me see her for a whole year, so whatever you got going on, leave me out of it," she said before hanging up in my face. I wanted to scream. I had to think of something. My last resort was calling Luke, but I guess it wouldn't hurt to try.

I called him, and he shut that shit down fast. I laid on my floor for hours, mad at myself for talking so much. I had heard him tell Keys he had a way for them to get some extra money, so I knew I couldn't return without Joi.

I needed to get high; that was the only way I would be able to think. I got up and went to find my purse. I couldn't think of where I had thrown it when I had come into the house. I always kept a little blow in my compact mirror for when he was acting funny with his shit. I was happy as hell when I opened the compact mirror and saw that I had enough for three lines. I took the first line, and my mind started rolling. I jumped in my car and headed to Luke's mom's house. It was the weekend, so I knew she would be there with her.

It was late night, so I knew my plan was going to work. I pulled into her driveway after I cut my lights off. I thought about parking down the street, but I didn't want to take a chance on someone hearing Joi yell. That baby knows she could wake up a whole neighborhood.

Since I knew Joi was probably in her room, I went to the back of the house. Luke's mom made his old room Joi's room. One thing I knew about that room was that the window didn't lock.

"So, you were gonna just handle this without my help?" Tory barked, scaring the shit out of me. I looked around, trying to figure out where the hell his ass had come from.

"Tory, what are you doing here?" I whispered.

"I pulled up to ya crib and was gonna scare the shit out of you, but when I saw you coming out, I decided to follow you." I was so fucking annoyed. I did not want him doing this with me, but since he was here, I figured we'd better hurry up and get this done. I went to the bathroom window and prayed I could fit through it. I knew I wouldn't be able to get out of it so I would have to use her bedroom window to exit.

"Why you looking confused? Ya little crackhead ass can fit in that window. When you get in, let me in through another window." I rolled my eyes and sucked my teeth.

"Tory, why can't you just wait in the car?"

"Meia, I ain't waiting in no damn car. Plus, this is Luke's mama's house, so there's probably so much shit in here we can take."

"Tory, I am not robbing his mother. That was not in the plan." He pulled his gun out and placed it at the center of my back.

"You gon' do what the fuck I say, or all three of y'all will die tonight."

"OK, meet me at the next window so I can let you in," I said a little under a whisper. The bathroom window was unlocked. I slid in, praying no one was on the toilet when I opened the curtains. The bathroom door was open, and I could see the light from the TV in the den. I then ran to the room that was next to the bathroom, which was Luke's mom's room, and she wasn't in there, so I assumed she had fallen asleep in the den, as usual. Once I made sure everything was clear, I opened the window for Tory. It was a good thing Luke's mom was still in the den sleeping because if not, this wouldn't be easy. After double checking she was still asleep, I headed to the room Joi was in with Tory trailing close behind me.

"Meia, is that you?" I heard Luke's mom's voice. *FUCK!* I thought she was sleeping.

"Mama, please just go lay back down. I decided to come get Joi for a couple of days."

"Meia, Luke didn't tell me anything like that, and who is this man you got in my house? How the fuck did y'all get in here?"

"Listen, lady, go the fuck back in that room where you were, and mind ya damn business."

"Nigga, that's my granddaughter, and she is my business." Tory pulled his gun out, and my eyes grew big as shit.

"Tory, what the fuck are you doing?"

"Meia, shut the fuck up and go get in the car."

"No, I will not leave and let you hurt her."

"You will do what I said, or I will kill ya daughter, then her, and let you live." He didn't have to tell me twice. I headed straight to the door, but before I left, I begged him not to kill her.

"If I hear that car peel off, she's as good as dead. Now go wait for me like I told you to." The minute I stepped on the step, I heard, *pop, pop.* The tears rolled down my face instantly, and all I could think was, *What did I get myself into?* I hurried and ran to the car before Joi woke up. My baby must have been tired because she was out and hadn't woken up yet. I was in the car, crying my heart out. The car door opened, and Tory jumped in with Luke's mom's purse and some of her jewelry.

"Did you kill her, Tory?"

"No, the bitch will live. She was doing too much slick talking, so I smacked her ass around a little."

"Tory, I heard gunshots
"She'll be OK!" he snapped and started the car up and peeled off.

"Tory, we weren't supposed to do that. Luke is going to go crazy."

"FUCK LUKE! I'm so fucking tired of hearing about him."

"I have to call him and tell him to get to his mama to get her some help."

"If you call him, I'm going to kill you and your daughter, now fuck with me if you want to."

I sat in the car and continued to cry my heart out. I had to figure out a way to call Luke to get to his mama.

Luke

The house was so fucking peaceful, but I missed Shawnee and Joi. I hoped Shawnee came home asap. I wanted to call her and tell her ass that I was sick so she could come home. I got out of bed and showered. I knew what I was going to put on, so that took no time.

I was cleaned up and ready to run the streets. When I got in the car, I called Keys so I could see what was up with him.

"What's good, boss man?" he joked. He knew I didn't like that shit, and that was why he did it.

"Shit, just checking. Where ya at?" I asked as I pulled out of my driveway.

"At the warehouse. Me and Cash just pulled up," he advised me. I was digging his work ethic. He was all about the money, up bright and early every day.

"OK. Cool, I'm headed that way," I told him before ending the call. I rolled a blunt while I was on the way since I hadn't had one before my shower. I got there in no time since I didn't live far. Keys was in the warehouse, giving orders, and Cash was in his office, so I headed in there with him.

"Shit, Keys keep moving like this, nigga, and we can retire asap," I laughed as I closed the door to his office.

"Damn right. I think I'm going to promote him again," Cash said as he ran money through the money machine. "Shit, sales been going up, and we don't have to deal with the little niggas. Hell, how did we skip over him and choose Dre?"

"I don't know, but what's done is done," I added. I lit the blunt and took a seat. I was sitting so I could see Keys talking to the workers. Cash cut on the PA system so we could hear what was going on.

"I miss my wife, nigga. Kyndall being gon' is in the fucking way. You have to bring her ass home 'cause I don't think I can take Shawnee being gone like this, and you know every time Kyndall is gone she'll be gone." I was fussing like a bitch. I didn't care, though. Hell, I wanted my baby home with me. A nigga was hungry as hell. Shit, she had breakfast ready every morning, and I missed that shit.

"Shit, I miss Kyndall, too, but I need to get shit in order first. Hell, I gotta at least get Nadia out my mom's house first."

"Kyndall gon' kill yo' ass."

"Who you telling? You know Moms fucks with Kyndall the long way, so I know that little relationship she built with Nadia gon' go right out the window. Hell, you know all y'all Team Kyndall, so Nadia has no chance."

Once he was done counting the money, I closed the blinds so he could put it in the safe. No one knew where the safe was but he and I. Honestly, it was in plain sight, but that smart-ass nigga had found a way to hide it.

"Call Keys in here. I don't know about you, but I wanna lay under my girl." I was all for that. I jumped up and opened the door fast as hell.

"Yo, Keys. Come let us holla at ya," I yelled. He set the bag down he was holding and headed towards us. When we walked in, Cash gestured for him to sit down. I went and stood by Cash.

"I just want to let you know that we see you working and we appreciate that shit. I got an opportunity for you if you open to it," Cash said as he sat on the edge of his desk.

"Y'all know I'm ready for whatever. I just wanna get some money so I can take care of my family."

"By the way, how is your girl doing?" I asked.

"She's OK, just taking it one day at a time. Shit, I'm ready for her to get well so I can put another baby in her," he joked.

"OK, so we need to head out of town for a day or two. Do you think you can hold shit down while we're gone?" His eyes lit up.

"Yea, I got y'all. I've been waiting for a chance to prove myself."

"Good, the only thing is, I don't want that nigga you be with around my shit. I trust you, Keys, and that's not normal. Show me you can handle shit, and we can talk about a promotion," Cash added. We talked about a few more things, then we headed out.

I went home to pack a small bag, and Cash did the same. Within an hour, we were headed to the airstrip. I couldn't wait to see my baby's face. My dick was getting hard just thinking about her ass.

■ ■

Three Hours Later…

"Nigga, wake up, we here," Cash said, shaking my shoulder.

"Damn, nigga, you didn't have to shake a nigga like that. What, are you trying to give me shaken baby syndrome or some shit? I'm going to have to watch CJ around yo' ass," I fussed as I got up.

"Really?"

"Fuck you mean, really? Hell yea. You gon' have a nigga head hurting doing that shit. Wait till I tell Shawnee."

"Go ahead. I'll just tell her yo' ass was dreaming about a female, and you were calling her name in ya sleep, so who will she be madder at?" he spat, grabbing his duffle bag.

"So we going that low? I'll just tell Kyndall about Nadia, then we'll see who's mad." He stopped walking and gave me an evil-ass look, and I burst out laughing. This nigga looked like he was going to cry.

"Fuck you," was all he said before walking off as I laughed my ass off. I grabbed my bag and followed him to a waiting SUV.

"We need to stop and get them something to eat. Ain't no way we can pop up on two pregnant females with no food; that's like a death threat. I don't know about you, but I wanna live," I told him as we pulled off from the airport lot. He told the driver to stop at The Cheesecake Factory, then pulled a blunt out of the console.

"My nigga," I joked. Cash always knew what a nigga needed. There was no feeling like waking up to a fat-ass blunt.

While he lit the blunt, I called and ordered their food so it would be ready when we got there. Thirty minutes later, we pulled up to the house they were living in, and I was amazed. That motherfucker was huge.

"Damn, the homegirl, living good. I think this motherfucker might be bigger than mine."

"Hell naw, nigga, yo' shit the size of a small island," he said while laughing. He wasn't lying, though. My shit was huge.

As soon as the truck stopped, we jumped out and headed towards the door. Cash knocked, and their homegirl answered.

"Hey, Danni! What's going on, crazy? Where's Kyndall?" Cash asked while pulling baby girl in for a hug. I guessed they had heard his voice, so they both ran to the door. The minute we got in the house, Shawnee jumped in my arms, and Kyndall pulled Cash in for a hug and kiss.

"I missed you so much, Luke."

"I missed ya sexy ass, too." I kissed her forehead, nose, then lips. The minute we were getting into a heated lip-locking session, my phone rang. The number was unknown, but I still picked up in case it was a work issue.

"Yo, who this?"

"Luke, Mama is hurt. You have to go check on her right now!" Meia screamed through the phone.

"What the fuck you talking about, Meia?" I barked into the phone, but all I heard was a dial tone. I didn't know what was going on, but if something had happened to my mama, where the fuck was my baby?

Chapter One

Meia

I had no idea where the hell Tory was taking us. I thought that he would take us back to my house or his house, but we were some fucking where on the outskirts of town. I was scared as hell. I wish there was a way that I could call Luke, but this nigga was on my ass. I prayed that he would leave us alone because that would give me time to call him. I powered my phone off when he was still in Luke's mom's house. I knew that if he would have seen or heard it he would have taken it. I slipped it in Joi's backpack. I knew that he wouldn't go in there.

We had been riding for at least an hour. For a minute, I didn't think that he knew where he was going. Hell, he probably didn't; his high done wore down so now he got his mind in order.

"Baby, where are we going?" I asked praying that he would tell me so when I called Luke I could tell him where we were. I had a feeling he was going to get on some dumb shit. Especially if his ass can't get high.

We pulled up to a gas station and I was happy as hell. I knew this would give me a chance to call Luke. I had my hand in my pocket powering the phone back on. That way soon as he got out I could call him.

"I will be back. Don't be stupid Meia."

Soon as he got out I pulled out my phone and dialed Luke. I cut the volume all the way down so that if he walked up he couldn't hear me. I had it on speaker; I was praying that he would answer. I knew that he probably wouldn't though. I was so relieved when I heard his voice.

"Yo, who this?" he answered. My heart was beating out of my chest because I could see Tory at the counter. Which meant that he would be coming out the door.

"Luke, Mama is hurt. You have to go check on her right now!" I screamed. I hoped that he understood me because I wasn't able to repeat myself.

"What the fuck you talking about, Meia?" I wanted to give him more details, but I knew that wasn't going to happen since Tory was coming out of the store. I ended the call and powered my phone back off as he was getting back in the car. I slipped my phone in my pocket just in time.

"Don't ask me where we are going anymore. You will see when we get here," was all he said.

I just sat back and took in everything that we passed. I was happy that my high had worn off because I would be able to take care of Joi. I knew that she was going to act a fool when she woke up and realized that she was with me. I knew that she hated to be around me. That shit hurt though. She was my baby and she loved his bitch ass girlfriend way more than she loved me.

I was so into my thoughts that I had stopped paying attention to where we were going. "Fuck," I mumbled.

"What the fuck you say that for?" he asked as he slowed and pulled into a driveway. I took note of the address even though I didn't know the street name.

"Nothing, I forgot her cup," I lied. I looked down at my baby and she was still sleeping. I knew that she must have really been tired. My baby was so pretty. Sometimes, I would look at her and wonder how did I make something so beautiful. At that moment, I knew that I needed to get my baby away from this crazy motherfucker. Something told me that he was going to be on some stupid shit.

"I know you lying but I'mma let it slide. Get out and don't try anything stupid Meia. I don't want to have to kill you." He must had been reading my mind because I was going to run soon as my feet touched the ground. I just took a deep breath and got my baby out the car. He waited at the front of the car for me so that he could walk ahead of me. When we made it to the door, he pulled out some keys like this was his home. I was in disgust when we walked in because the house was a damn mess on the inside. It was a decent looking house that had potential, but it just needed to be cleaned. I walked to the back to find a clean spot to lay Joi down. Once I found one, I pulled my phone out and powered it on then slipped it in Joi's bag. Soon as I had a chance, I was going to send Luke my location.

"Give me your phone." He scared the shit out of me. That meant that he was sober. *Fuck.* I pulled out my phone and handed it to him. Now I had to rethink my plan. I knew that he was no dumb ass, especially when he was sober. I handed him my phone regretting not deleting the call that I made to Luke. I knew that he was goin' to go through the phone. I just prayed that he didn't kill me or my baby.

After I got my thoughts a little situated, I decided to take a tour of the house. I could tell that no one had been here in a while. There were spider webs everywhere. The kitchen table was full of old food containers and beer cans, and the trash smelled terrible. After gagging and holding my stomach from the smell I headed back into the room where I laid Joi down and sat next to her. Just looking at her I knew that I had really fucked up. I couldn't believe I let my hate for Luke put Joi in harm's way.

Luke

I had been calling Meia phone for the past hour, but I wasn't getting an answer. I called my mom and she wasn't answering either. I knew then that something was wrong. My mom never missed a call. She was like a teenager when it came to her phone. All she did was a scroll on Facebook.

"Fuck," I yelled. Everyone was on edge. Shawnee was pacing the floor. Kyndall was doing the same and Cash was smoking.

"Call Keys," Cash demanded. I did as he told me and handed him the phone. He put the phone on speaker and waited for keys to answer.

"What up Bruh," he answered.

"Aye, some shit done went down. I need you to go by Luke mom spot. I'm going to send you the address. Call me soon as you get there," Cash instructed.

"Alright. I'm on it."

Soon as he ended the call with him, I grabbed Shawnee and walked out the door. There was no way that I was going to just sit here. I looked back and Cash and Kyndall were walking out the door followed by Danni. I jumped in the rental and pulled off once everyone was in the truck.

"My pilot is waiting for us on the runway," Cash advised. I just nodded and headed to the airport. All that was on my mind was making sure that my mom and baby were good. I was going to kill Meia ass, as soon as I laid eyes on her because I knew that she was the cause of this.

Just as we were pulling to the airstrip my phone rang and it was Keys. I answered on speaker.

"Yo you need to get back asap," he advised. I knew that shit was bad. "I'm headed to the hospital. I will hit y'all when I get there," was all he said before hanging up. Hell, I didn't get a chance to ask what was going on. And honestly, I think that he did that shit on purpose.

I didn't realize that tears were flowing until I felt Shawnee's soft hand rub down my face. It was something about the way that she made me feel when she touched me. "Luke we are going to find our baby. Don't worry."

We all boarded the plane and headed back to Camden. I knew that the flight was going to seem long because I was so ready to get back. All I could think about was my baby and my mama. It was something about the way that Keys sounded that didn't sit right with me.

Once the plane finally took off, I did my best to drift off to sleep so that the time would go by fast, but I couldn't. My mind was all over the place. All that I could think about was how Meia knew that something was going on with my mama. That let me know that whatever had happened she had something to do with it. I was getting to the point that I hated her. If I found out that she had my baby and hurt my mom I was going to kill her ass with my bare hands.

"Aye bruh, let me holla at ya," Cash demanded, pulling me from my thoughts. I lifted Shawnee up and placed a pillow under her sleeping head. My baby was fucking beautiful. I couldn't wait to make her my wife.

We walked to the back of the plane. I could tell by the look on his face that he was about to tell me something that was going to piss me off more.

"I was thinking about that call that you got so I emailed my tech guy and had him to trace where the call came from. He said that the call came from almost an hour away from the city. He wasn't able to trace the number so she must have powered her phone off," he explained. The wheels were turning in my head. I knew that she didn't know many people, so she had to be with some nigga. That was her weakness. She would fall dumb behind a nigga. I never saw a woman that would do whatever for the attention of a nigga. That had always been an issue with Meia. Shit, she was like that with me. Whatever I said she did it. I remember before she got pregnant, I told her to set this nigga up because he owed me some money. She did that shit without a second thought.

"Well that bitch is dead anyway, so it doesn't matter. She better hope whatever nigga she with kills her because I'm going to make sure that she die a long painful death." After we talked for a while longer, I headed back to my seat. Before I knew it, I had drifted off.

***

"Baby, wake up; we here." Soon as I heard Shawnee say that I jumped up. The plane's doors were already open, so I headed down the steps. I waited for everyone to get in the car. I knew that Kyn wasn't supposed to be on a plane, so I made sure that she was good before we pulled off. The first stop that I was making was to check on my mama.

We pulled to the front door of the hospital and let the women out then parked. I was happy that we did that because I needed to make some calls. I called a meeting and Cash called the tech guy. I need to find my baby asap. There was no telling what they would do to her and that thought alone had me ready to paint the city red.
Once we got checked in, they took me straight to my mom. Keys was sitting in the chair next to her. She was hooked up to all kinds of shit. That shit broke my heart. I made my way over to her with my baby following behind me. I grabbed her hand and she grabbed mine back. I wanted to ask so many questions, but I knew this wasn't the time.
I nodded for Keys to follow me out the door. I knew that Cash was coming so there was no need for me to say anything to him. Soon as we made it in the hall he began to tell me what was going on. That shit angered me. Meia was going to have to see me.

Chapter Two

Keys

The whole time that I was at the hospital Tory had been blowing my damn phone up. I knew damn well that nigga didn't want shit. I had been lying telling him that I hadn't been getting money with Luke and Cash because I knew that he would start leeching. The other day he asked me to borrow some money and that wasn't going to happen; he was my nigga and I would hate to have to kill his ass.

"What's good?" I answered as he called once again.

"Nigga, I got some shit for us. Nigga this a major hit," he told me sounding happy as hell. What he didn't know was that I wasn't hurting for money. I honestly had more than I knew what to do with. You would never know that looking at me because I wasn't a flashy nigga. I was low-key. Hell, Chrissy didn't even know how paid I was.

"I'm listening." I was doing my best to mask my irritation. I really had better things that I could have been doing rather than wasting my time with him. On top of doing shit for Cash and Luke, I needed to find out what had happened to Dre and where that nigga Keem was. I knew that more than likely Dre was dead 'cause he always stayed on that snake shit, but Keem I knew nobody's mind was on him but mine. I wanted that nigga dead ASAP for what he did to Chrissy, and for the death of my unborn seed. Yeah, this nigga had to pay.

"You remember the house that I told you that I got when my granddaddy died?"

"Yea."

"Meet me there," was all that he said.

I really didn't have time for his shit, but I was going to see what he was talking about. I headed back in the hospital so that I could see if Luke needed anything before, I left. When I walked in the room, he handed me a picture of his daughter. She was a spitting image of that nigga. "Make copies and have as many soldiers as you can on the street. Find my baby girl; set an award. I don't give a fuck, just find her."

No words needed to be spoken. I just nodded and headed out the door. I knew how I would feel if it was my daughter, so I was going to do what was needed to make sure that I found his baby. I called a meeting for later and headed to see what was up with Tory.

When I got to the car, I realized that I had missed a call from Chrissy. I called back but didn't get an answer. I knew that she was probably just checking to see what I was doing. Her ass called all day. It's crazy that her and I are finally together. I would have never thought. I had been trying to get at her for years, but she wouldn't give me any play. I guess she wanted a square ass nigga.

Since she didn't pick back up, I headed to my crib to make sure she was ok. They had finally released her from the hospital the other day, and she was getting better. I noticed the depression coming on, so I made a vow that whenever she needed me, I would drop any and everything to make sure she was good.

A half hour later I was pulling up to my crib. I parked the car then jumped out. Once I opened my door, I heard soft music playing, and I smelled something cooking. I really didn't have time to chill, but for her, I would at least eat with her before I hit the streets. I walked into the kitchen and she was in front of the stove cooking and swaying from side to side listening to some old school shit. *It Had To Be You* by *Silk* played loudly while she sang. I couldn't do anything but laugh while watching her from the doorway.

You, I knew it had to be you
You turn my gray skies blue, I knew it had to be you
Listen, from the first day, I saw you girl
I knew you were the woman, to be in my world...

She turned around to go to the sink and saw me standing there smiling. I could tell I frightened her, 'cause of the way she jumped.

"Keys, why didn't you let me know you were standing there, boy; you scared the shit out of me." This was another reason I needed to find this cat Keem. I didn't need my girl always being scared and looking over her shoulders.

I walked up to her and pulled her in for a hug. Today she looked like she was in good spirits. Considering what she's been through. Yes, Chrissy has been on real bullshit, but being with a nigga like me I'mma make sure that ass changes her ways.

"My fault ma. I was just standing back watching you do ya thing. You must be feeling better today." I said while kissing her on her forehead.

"I actually am, so I figured I would get up and fix my man some lunch. Since he's always so damn busy."

"Thanks, baby! I really appreciate you. I was about to stop and get some bullshit cause Luke got me on a mission today. We have to find his little girl."

"Oh My God! I hope she's ok." Chrissy said with sad eyes.

"Me too for the sake of his baby mama. 'Cause if little mama ain't good Luke is going to lose it, and it ain't gone be no stopping him."

"Well, baby if you don't have time to sit with me, I understand. I'll just pack ya food up and you take it with you." Chrissy said sadly.

The way that sounded told me that she would be disappointed if I didn't eat with her. So, I was goin' to enjoy lunch with her. Then I would go handle my business. My phone started ringing, and I knew it was Tory's bitch ass. He was goin' to have to wait. I was doing this little lunch date with my shawty.

"Nope… I'm having lunch with my favorite girl then I'll go handle business. What did you make us?" I asked with a smile on my face.

"Homemade bacon cheeseburgers, french fries, with a pickle on the side. I also made some homemade strawberry lemonade." Chrissy cooed while bringing my plate over to me. Before she had a chance to walk away, I pulled her on my lap.

"Thank you, sweetheart!" I whispered in her ear while kissing her neck. I missed touching her sexy ass, but I knew sex was out of the question right now, which was fine with me. I would just wait until she was able to. I know y'all think I'm crazy for falling for Chrissy, but y'all don't understand I've loved her since before she became this person that everyone hates.

"Keys you're welcome baby... Now eat, so you can get back to work." She kissed my lips while getting up and grabbing her food so she could join me.

"You sure you good today?"

"Yes... I'm fine! I haven't experienced any pain yet today. I talked to my doctor this morning and I start counseling sessions next week. I think it'll help with everything that's goin' on in my life right now and also my past."

"Anything you need to do to get back to ya old self I'm all for it. I'll be here with you every step of the way. I love you Chrissy, and I mean that shit. Always have, always will."

"But why?" She asked just above a whisper and I was taken back by her question.

"What's not to love baby girl? Yeah, you got some issues, but who don't? I've always had a crush on you growing up. Then being cool with ya brother I was able to be around you often. As we grew up together my feelings got deeper, but of course, you weren't trying to deal with a nigga like me. The street nigga wasn't ya type, but you went out here and fell for a suit and tie cat and look how that shit turned out. You can't judge a book by its color baby. Now you wasted all these years not letting me show you how much I love you. Since I got you in my presence now, I'm never letting you go."

All the shit I was saying to her I meant. I finally had her, and I wasn't letting her go at all. The shit that she's been on, I already know, but when the time is right I'mma sit down and talk to her about it. Like dude killing Dre; I knew that wasn't true. I had already known that Luke and Cash had something to do with Dre. I heard that nigga was stealing from them which is why he's dead. I'm hurt by it, but that nigga shouldn't have been on that snake shit. I needed to find out why she lied about it though.

Tory

Keys was on real bullshit. I had been waiting for him for hours now. Shit, if he didn't want in on this he could have just let me know. Word around the streets is that he mess with that stuck up ass chick we went to school with. He has been after her ass for years, but if he is gone let her mess up the money he needs to let that ass go.

"Tory, can we please take her back home. She misses her family." Meia cried.

"Bitch she ain't goin' no fucking where until we get that ransom money. My boy is on his way then when he gets here we gon' iron all this out. If everything goes as planned she'll be back in her father's arms between tonight and tomorrow."

"I'm so sick of this shit, Tory. This was not a good idea. We both are goin' to end up dead." I was sick of her mouth, so I walked up to her and slapped her right in the mouth, and she fell to the floor.

"Now shut the fuck up, before I do more than that." Meia laid on the floor crying with a busted lip, but I didn't give a fuck. She had been driving me crazy since we've been here. It had been a couple of days since all this went down, and to be honest I was sick of waiting. Which is why I called Keys 'cause I knew that nigga would have a plan.

"Tory… you said you wouldn't hit me while my daughter was here."

"You said you were goin' to stop all that damn nagging but did you stop. No, now go clean ya face for little mama come in here crying. I'm sick of her ass too." I snapped while heading back into the kitchen. Meia got up and walked back into the room with her daughter and slammed the door. My phone went off alerting me that I had a text message. I grabbed it and it was Keys letting me know he was out front. I jumped up and went to answer the door.

"Yo, bro… What's good with you? Why have you been calling me like crazy? You know my girl just got out of the hospital, so I been off the radar lately."

"My fault yo. I didn't even know all that was goin' on. But check this; come on in and let me rap to you real quick."

He walked in looking around all strange. For some reason, he seemed off a little. Not like the Keys I used to run the streets with. But I was still goin' to let him in on my plans.

"So, what's up with this money move you speaking on?"

"Well, you know them niggas Cash and Luke right?"

"Yeah, what about them?"

"I fucks with Luke's baby mama heavy, and we came up with a scheme to get some money out of him. We got his daughter here and we trying to figure out how much of a ransom to ask for. I mean them niggas got dough; they been running shit out here for a minute." Keys chuckled while stroking his beard.

"Nigga, you really kidnapped the little girl?"

"Well, it's technically not kidnapping. I am fucking the mama." We both burst out laughing.

"I guess you right, where they at now?" He asked.

"They in the back chilling. So, what you think? Help me figure this shit out."

"For starters, you need a master plan. 'Cause I heard that nigga will go batshit crazy over that little girl. So, what was your plan before you decided to call me?"

"I was goin' to get her to call, but I don't think he will take her serious."

"Nah… he probably won't. But what I do know is if he gets a hold of y'all he gone kill y'all. So, you have to be smart about ya next move." Keys assured me.

"That's why I called you. 'Cause I know you're the best."

"Check this; lay low until tomorrow, and when I come back we gon' have everything in motion. You know I got you, and here goes a couple of dollars for right now in case little mama needs to eat. Remember what I said, lay low my nigga. I got you bright and early tomorrow morning."

"Ok… I got you but if you don't come back in the morning, I'm goin' to do this shit on my own," I assured him.

"I told you I got you." Keys pleaded. The room door opened and Meia came out.

"I thought I told you to stay ya ass in the room," I yelled and she jumped.

"Tory, I have to get Joi something to drink. I don't understand why you always gotta holler at me like I'm a small child." She sassed while rolling her eyes.

"See, you always talking shit. You just got ya ass smacked for that shit not even an hour ago, and you still mouthing off." I snapped.

"Come on, bro, I know you ain't hittin that girl with her seed here." Keys asked with a raised brow.

"My nigga, that's my bitch. I do what the fuck I wanna do with her. Babe, you wanna make a couple of dollars." I asked with a thought in my mind.

"Doing what?" Meia asked while looking over at me.

"Go suck my boy dick real quick in the back room." Meia looked at me with wide eyes, but she knew she better do what the fuck I said.

"Come on, man, you don't even have to be on that." Keys refused.

"Man, go ahead while I'm giving you permission." After turning me down a couple more times, Keys eventually got up and followed Meia to the back room. I brought him in on a money move and he, about to get a good dick sucking. He shouldn't have any problem with coming back to help me.

Fifteen minutes later, Keys and Meia came walking out of the bathroom. Meia looked strange, but Keys was all smiles. I wonder what her problem was.

"Did you do that thing with ya mouth baby?" I asked while laughing. Meia was in her feelings but I didn't give a damn.

"Alright my nigga. I got to get out of here, but I definitely will be back in the morning. Oh, and thanks little mama; you do the damn thing with that mouth."

"See that's why I keep her around. Did you pay her?"

"Of course I did; you know not to ask me some shit like that."

"Alright, I'm just making sure. Come on and get ya ass out of here. And make sure you on time in the morning."

"Nigga, it ain't no damn timeframe. But you know I get up early as shit." Keys gloated.

I walked him to the door and watched him pull off. I then locked up the house and headed to the couch to sit my ass down to relax. I finally felt like my plan was in motion. I just hoped that Keys comes through like he promised.

Chapter Three

Meia

I couldn't believe that Tory sent me in the room with this nigga. I really didn't know him for Tory to be telling me to the suck his dick. Soon as the door was closed, he threw me to the wall.

"You that hard up that you would put your child in danger. You know what type of nigga Tory is; he doesn't give a fuck about you or Joi," he gritted. I knew that what he was saying was true but I wasn't thinking right. I should have thought of another way to get money from Luke other than putting Joi in danger. That was dumb on my part.

"I was high. I wasn't thinking straight," I admitted. If I got out of this shit, I was getting clean. There is no way that I could live my life like this.

"Well, you are going to have to pay for that shit. You should know Luke better than anyone. That nigga is not wrapped tight," he laughed. I flopped down on the bed because I knew that what he was saying was true. Luke was going to kill my ass soon as he laid eyes on me.

"But look I'm going to get y'all out of here. I can't say if he will kill you or not. Just make sure that he doesn't touch her. I have been knowing that nigga a long time, and I know how he gets down. You need to take all the heat so that he doesn't think about harming Joi. I will be back. Just know that if you tell him what we talked about things will be worse. I'm going to try and help but don't make me regret it. When we walk out I'm going to act as if you gave me head. Take the few dollars so that he won't get suspicious." He peeled off two hundred-dollar bills and handed them to me.

"What if he suspects something," I asked.

"He won't. I'm going to give y'all something so that he won't be paying attention. Suck and fuck that nigga till he falls asleep." He explained. I just nodded because I knew that he knew what he was doing.

I let him walk out first because I wanted to make sure that my face was right. He was sober so he would be able to read my face. I also made sure that I had the money in my hand. I wanted him to see it.

Once Keys was gone Tory made a few phone calls. I was doing my best to read in between the lines but I couldn't. I had given my baby some benadryl so that she could sleep. I wanted to make sure she was out of his way at all times. I heard Keys say that he would be back in the morning but that wasn't a guarantee. A part of me was ready for this shit to be over.

I got up and went to check on my baby. When I walked in the room, she was sound asleep, looking like a doll. Her hair was in the cutest braids. I knew that Luke's girlfriend had to have done them because his mama wasn't that good at combing hair. A smile crept on my face knowing that my baby would be in good hands with Luke and Shawnee. I was really happy that he had her because Joi needed a mother figure in her life.

"What you doing?" Tory asked, scaring me.

"Nothing, just checking on her."

"Come here and get high with me." I knew that I didn't need to be high but there was no way that I was going to tell this crazy ass nigga no.

I followed him to the living room. There were ten lines waiting. I didn't know where he got the dope from but I was all for it. I knew that it would only take me a few lines and I would be good. I wanted him to have the most because I knew that he would be high and fall to sleep.

"Damn baby," I said as I made my way to the table.

"Go take one baby," he told me. I did as he told me, and I swear I needed that shit. I felt like I had energy. I looked at him as he took one as well. If I knew him like I thought I did then I knew that he was on his third one. I looked at him and his dick was rock hard just like always. I made my way to him. My shit was dripping wet. That's what that dope did to me.

"Come suck this dick," he demanded. I damn near ran to his ass. "Just like that bitch," he moaned as I swallowed his shit whole.

When I was high, I was a whole other person. I was sucking him off like my life depended on it. Hell, it really did. Once he nutted, I knew that he would want some pussy. Good thing that I was clean. He hated when my shit had a smell. I got up to undress. Just as I was finishing there was a knock at the door. I knew that it wasn't Keys because he had just left so I was puzzled.

He got up to open the door. It was an older White guy. He looked like he was a truck driver or something by the way that he was dressed. He made his way in the house. And I was trying to figure out what was going on.

"Yall can go in the room back there," he said to the guy. There was only one room in this house and that was the room that my baby was in, so I knew damn well he didn't think I was going to fuck in the room with my baby. He had really lost his damn mind.

"What are we going back there for?" I asked.

"So that you can make us some money until this lick comes through. This shit will be gone before the night is out," he said pointing to the dope that was on the table. "Now hurry up because you got a few more coming."

When he said that I vomited in my mouth. I didn't sell pussy and if he thought that he might as well kill my ass now. I just stood there looking at him. "You can go, or I can find some sick ass niggas that like little girls." I damn near ran when he said that. I went into the room and covered my baby's face up with the blanket that was on her. I didn't want her to wake up and see me like this. Since I was already naked, I laid on my back and let this big nasty motherfucker have his way with me. I felt so nasty. It was taking everything in me not to vomit on him. I was no longer high; I was sober as hell. His penis was small, but I was in so much pain because I was bone dry. I hated Tory at this very moment.

Chrissy

Shit had been super crazy lately. The pain and the nightmares were ready to take my ass over. I needed to call to get some type of counseling sessions going. Ever since the day Dre's wife confronted me about him dying being my fault. I've been having nightmares. It seems like every time I close my eyes I either see Dre or Keem. The crazy part about all of this is will Keys still love me after he finds out the truth about the shit I did?

Like, I can't believe I went through so much to be with a man who didn't want me. A man that tried to kill my ass. I was hoping and praying that Keem's ass was dead somewhere. 'Cause I was still scared for my life.

I wanted to come clean about everything, but then I figured I would take that shit to my grave. I know I did some fucked up shit, but I'm trying to be a changed woman. I lost my baby and my brother behind all this bullshit. Not to mention, I was growing to love Keys. The feeling of loving someone and them, loving you back was every bit of amazing.

After getting up early cleaning and fixing Keys' lunch, the pain was finally starting to kick in. I wanted to take some pain pills, but I was trying not to. I didn't wanna get addicted to them. They have seemed to be my best friend to help me sleep, and I felt like I was starting to take too many.

Once Keys left out, I cleaned the kitchen, and now my body is paying for it. I decided to head up to my room and run me a hot bath and throw some Epsom salt in the water. While I was in the bathroom, I looked in the mirror and noticed my scars were clearing up. Keem really did a number on me. The way drugs make a person turn it's really crazy. Thinking about all of this made sadness come over me all of a sudden. The loss of my son was the worst day of my life, and I feel so bad for Keys. I knew for sure this was his baby, but I wanted it to be Keem's so bad. I was still so lost on to why Keys loves a person like me. I had issues, and I needed help.

Since I knew that Keys would be gone for a while, I decided that I would soak and then get me a nap in. The house was so quiet when he was gone. Once I was done in the bathroom, I climbed into the bed. It had been a while since I read so I decided that I would find a book to read until I fell asleep. Reading helped me cope with life. There was always so much going on and I needed an outlet.

Just as I was getting into my book my phone rang. I saw that it was my sister in law, so I hit ignore. I didn't feel like talking to her ass. All she was going to do was question me about my brother. I was trying to move on from that. She should have been trying to do the same. She knew the type of nigga that my brother was. That was part of the reason that my mama wasn't tripping on his death. It was bound to happen sooner or later. My brother had been into all kinds of shit when we were growing up. I remember one time he tried to steal from my mama boyfriend. When she confronted Dre, his ass went and told my uncle that the nigga pulled a gun on him. So, as you know my uncle bodied his ass. Dre acted like nothing happened. I knew then that his ass wasn't shit.

I wanted to just power my phone off, but I knew that Keys might call. He would call randomly just to check on me. That was one of the things that I loved. No matter how busy he was he made sure that he checked in with me.

I had finally gotten comfortable as someone knocked at the door. I just laid there because Keys didn't want me opening the door when he wasn't home. I called him but didn't get an answer. So, I just let whoever was knocking knock. I closed the bedroom door so that I could get some rest until he got back.

Ring... Ring...

I rolled my eyes because once again my phone woke me out of my sleep. I wanted to throw this damn phone across the room. When I looked and saw that it was my baby calling back, I got happy as hell.

"Hey baby," I answered.

"What's up? You called?" he asked. I could tell that something was on his mind, but I didn't want to ask. He would get mad when I did that, so I just kept my thoughts to myself.

"Yes, someone came by. I didn't go to the door or look to see who it was."

"Ok, I will look at the cameras and see who it was when I get in. You good though? I got some shit I'm finna go and handle. I will be home soon as I'm done," he told me. That caused a smile to creep on my face. That was all that I needed to hear.

"Ok baby, I'm finna lay down. I will see you when you get here. Be careful," I told him before ending the call.

Since it had been a while since I talked to my mother, I decided that I would call and see what she was doing. I knew that she was going to curse me out because I had been avoiding her ever since my brother went missing. I think it was the guilt that I was feeling. I knew that she would question me and that was something that I was not ready for. My mama was always team Dre. No matter what he did in her eyes he was always right.

I took a deep breath before hitting the call button. The phone rang for what seemed like forever. "I know this ain't my runaway ass daughter calling me," she answered.

"Hey, Mama!"

"Don't hey me lil girl. You got me around here going crazy worried about you." I was shocked because I really didn't think that she cared that much. My mama was a tough love parent. She would curse our ass out in a hot second and wouldn't care how we felt about it. That was part of the reason my skin was so tough.

"Sorry Mama," I replied. She went on telling me all the family gossip. But she had yet to say anything about Dre. "Y'all still haven't heard from Dre?" I asked just to see where her head was.

"No, you know how yo brother is. He probably got into some shit that he couldn't get out of. That damn wife of his been calling all day every day like some shit gone change. I don' stressed about that damn boy so much that I just gave up. Hell, I'm not getting any younger. I'm trying to live life. He will pop back up like he always does," she explained. "But what has been going on with you?"

"Oh My God Mama! Life is finally good. I have a man that loves me. He treats me like the queen that you always told me that I was."

"That's good baby. I'm happy for you. Who is this man? And when am I going to meet him?"

"Well, you kind of already met him," I told her.

"I hope you not talking about that damn married man that you work for." I knew that she would say that. She hated Keem. She said that it was something weird about him and that was before she knew that he was married.

"No Mama! It's Keys," I beamed. I was so happy that I gave him a chance. I never knew that I could be this happy.

"I knew he was going to get yo ass. That boy has been trying forever. I'm so happy for you baby. You need to come to the house soon. I miss you and I need to lay eyes on you," my mother told me. We talked for a while longer and then we ended the call. I laid in the bed and just smiled. Life was finally good for me.

Chapter Four

Luke

My mind was in a million places. There was no way that this shit was happening to me. I had been at the hospital since we landed. My mom was still in surgery and I had no fucking idea where my daughter was. That shit was killing me. I was their protector and I wasn't there to protect them. I looked around the room and everyone was in a daze. I knew deep down Shawnee was having a fit. She wanted to take Joi with her, but I told her that she could just stay with my mom. I was regretting that shit now. I just prayed that nothing had happened to my baby. I went and sat in between Shawnee and Kyndall. They both looked like they wanted to kill someone. I wish that I wouldn't have brought them because they didn't need to be stressing the babies out, especially Kyndall.

"Y'all go and get something to eat in the cafeteria," I told the both of them. They looked like they wanted to say something, but they just took the money that I pulled out and did as I said. Soon as they walked off Keys walked up. There was a look on his face that I couldn't read.

"We gotta go," was all that he said. I pulled out my phone to call Shawnee to tell her that I had to leave. Once she told me that she was on the way back up, I told the girl at the desk that I was gone, and they were headed back. When I walked out the door, Cash had that look on his face, so I knew what was up. Once we all were in the car Keys pulled off. We made it down the street from the warehouse and he pulled over. "I found Joi and Meia." That had me looking at him crazy. Why didn't he tell us this at the hospital?

"So why didn't you tell us at the hospital?" Cash asked as if he was reading my mind.

"I didn't want to say nothing in front of all them motherfuckers. But I will say this, I'm not a fuck nigga. I see ya face, so I know what y'all thinking. If I was a fuck nigga, I wouldn't be going against a nigga that I have known since the sandbox days," he explained.

I knew that had to be some hard shit to do since we had just met a few years back. He was a thorough nigga. That was part of the reason that he was on my team.

"So, take me to my baby." That was all that needed to be said. After riding for nearly an hour we pulled on the side of the road. He looked at me and I knew he was finna say some crazy shit.

"Look, I need to know if you ok with yo baby moms dying." I had to think for a second. She was Joi's mother. I knew that the drugs had her doing this crazy shit but at the same time she was grown; she made the decision for herself. She knew what would happen the moment that she took my baby and allowed that nigga to hurt my mother. For that, she had to die no questions asked.

"Murk that bitch," was all that I said before we got out the car.

"Wait, man… chill a second. Now come on Luke think about this bro. Yeah, she fucked up, but you know it's the drugs. If you kill her you're going to hurt Joi. She may have fucked up, but my goddaughter loves her mama. So, what you should do is off that nigga and make her get some fucking help. If she doesn't stay clean, then you let that bitch go. But don't kill her 'cause Joi loves her." Cash said looking at me with a straight face. I gave him a crazy ass look 'cause I really didn't wanna spare her life, but I would do anything for my princess.

"Alright man… I'll let her live, but I'm not gone promise y'all I'm not gone smack her stupid ass around a couple of times."

"Ok cool… well, let's go; she's right up the road in this old ass house. My old boy Tory has her in here. He hit me up earlier wanting me in on this plan with him. He wanted me to help him figure out a ransom. When I saw it was your bm and daughter I put my thinking cap on right away. So, he thinks I'm coming back tomorrow to help. I couldn't wait a long time to come to get y'all cause this nigga is like a loose cannon. Especially when he can't get high. So, I made sure earlier to leave him some dope, and I told Meia to keep little mama away from him at all times. She really gone off the drugs. We talked for a little bit, and she told me when she made this decision, she was high out of her mind. So, I bet she didn't know until she was sober that she sold her soul to the devil. Now she has to do whatever that nigga says or she getting her ass beat. That nigga even made her take me to a room to suck my dick. Of course, that was my way of talking to her and letting her know that we were going to get lil' mama out of here. I already let her know that you were gone fuck her ass up."

"Yo, Luke we made a great decision putting this nigga on. I'm feeling his way of thinking. Man, you just may have got another promotion when this is all over." Cash assured me with a big ass smile on his face. He was right; Keys was a great choice to let join our team.

After bussing it up for a couple more minutes and Keys putting us up on game, we were now in front of the house. Once we made it up the front steps, we heard a whole lot of commotion that caused us all the pull out our guns. I tried the front door to see if we had to kick the mutha fucker down, but it was unlocked, I left Keys to see if Meia was still breathing. She was badly beaten and lying in a puddle of blood. He checked her pulse and gave me a head nod letting me know that she still had one. I gave Cash a look letting him know to handle that nigga, while I hurried and got Joi up out of the room. The minute I made into the living room of the house, I looked her over to make sure she was good.

"You good baby? Did anybody touch you?"

"No… daddy but the bad man hurt mommy. Is her dead daddy?" Joi asked while still crying.

"Baby, mommy is going to be fine. Daddy's friend is going to take her to the doctors." I assured her while carrying her in my arms holding her tight.

I didn't want her to see Keys carrying Meia out of the house or hearing Cash shoot Tory 'cause I knew that's exactly what he was going to do. So, I hurried down the street to Keys' car and jumped in. I sat in the back seat with Joi, and all I kept doing was looking her over and making sure she was straight. She was clean and her braids were still neat, so that showed me that Meia made sure she was straight. I knew she was going to have nightmares, and I was sure going to get her checked out as soon as we left here. The sound of Cash opening the car door brought me out of my thoughts.

"It's handled bro. I hit up the crew and told them to come to clean it up. I also told them to torch it since it looks like a trap house anyway. How's baby girl doing?" He asked in a concerned tone.

"She's going to be just fine; come on bro; let's get out of here." Cash did as he was told and we peeled off heading back to make sure my mama and the girls were straight.

Kyndall

Too much was going on and my little peanut was having a field day in my belly. I was starting to get a little concerned 'cause of how she was moving. Luke's mother had just got out of surgery and we just got the call that Joi was safe. We were so relieved; Shawnee and I had been so scared of what the outcome of this would be. My cousin was so hurt by the news about Joi and Luke's mama. She tried not to stress 'cause of the baby, but I knew she was hurting on the inside.

"Are you alright? I see you keep grabbing ya stomach."

"I'm good; this baby just keeps moving today for some reason."

"Don't lie to me Kyndall. You're right here in the hospital; if you need to get checked then do so. We all know your history and it's better to be safe than sorry."

"Shawnee… I swear I'm fine; the baby is just a little more active than usual; it's nothing unsafe about that." I assured her. Shawnee sucked her teeth and rolled her eyes. I wasn't paying her mean ass any mind though. She always swears she's the fucking boss. My phone rang, bringing me out of my thoughts.

"Shawnee, I'mma step in the hall. Mom-Mom is calling me." I picked up the phone as soon as I stepped foot in the hall.

"Hey, baby! How is everybody holding up?"

"Well, Luke's mama just came out of surgery and they say she's going to be just fine. Luke and Cash has Joi and they're on their way here to get her checked out."

"Ok… that's good news. How are you and Shawnee holding up?"

"We good Mom-Mom; just trying to be there for Luke and his family."

"Alright now. Y'all better make sure y'all feeding my grandbaby's and not doing too much stressing. And tell

Luke to bring me that baby if he needs to spend time with his mama. Shawnee and Joi can stay with me until everything is ok with his mother. I know most of his time is going to be spent up at that hospital the way he feels about his mama."

"Ok… Mom-Mom, I'll be sure to let him and Shawnee know."

"Alright, baby and remember what I said about stressing my grandbabies." I laughed at Mom-Mom 'cause she was going to drive Shawnee and me crazy about these damn kids.

As soon as I was about to walk back in the room I felt a sharp pain in my side. This wasn't normal, so I walked into the room to let Shawnee know. Ain't this some bullshit. I just told Mom-Mom I was good and now look.

I walked into the room and Shawnee was holding Luke's mama's hand. I hated to interrupt, but my ass was scared.

"Shawnee, I think I need to see a doctor. I felt a sharp pain in my side on my way back in here."

She jumped up so fast and ran over to me. Shawnee then grabbed my hand and led the way out of the door.

"I'm about to call Cash right now." I really didn't want her to call him and get him all scared. But I knew she wasn't going to pay me any mind. Before I even got a chance to object, her ugly ass had him on the phone. I sucked my teeth and walked up to the receptionist's desk. I explained to them what was going on and they immediately got me a wheelchair and took me straight to labor and delivery. Twenty minutes later, I was lying in a bed with all these monitors connected to my belly. The baby's heartbeat was going strong and she was still doing all this moving.

"Well, hello Mrs. Richardson! How have you been? I see you and Mr. Richardson didn't waste any time." The doctor that delivered Nevaeh walked into the room. Hearing her say that brought all sadness up. I know she didn't know, but still, at this very moment, I felt like shit. Shawnee looked at me and shook her head.

"Don't you dare get upset. This baby may not be by your husband, but it was made out of love. Doc, she is no longer with Mr. Richardson." Shawnee sassed while rolling her eyes.

"Oh My! I'm so sorry. I really didn't mean to upset you. But on a brighter side of things, this baby is fine, healthy, and strong. She is not trying to come into the world just yet. Whatever you ate today must have little mama active."

"Shawnee... look at me smiling. Did you say girl doc?"

"Oops... I'm just saying too much today." She chuckled.

"Oh no, you're fine doctor. Her little stubborn butt wouldn't let us see what she was. Every time we went to get the ultrasound done her legs would be closed."

"Oh ok... I see. Well, she's going to be something else. I can tell by all the moving around."

Cash came running into the room with a sad look in his eyes. He ran right over to the bed and kissed me right on my forehead.

"Baby... is everything ok?" He asked.

"Yes... the baby is fine. She just gave me a little scare. I guess it's too much going on around us."

Cash looked at the doctor for confirmation before he looked back at me.

"Yes... daddy, it's a girl, and she is doing fine and looking healthy. Mrs. Richardson's pressure is good, and her blood levels are good too. You're going to have a healthy baby but just not today. I would like for her to stay here for just another hour or two. Just to monitor her a little more to make sure there are no changes."

"Alright, doc... thanks a lot!" Cash said with a smile on his face.

"Hows Joi?"

"She's good for now. I think she's going to need some counseling, but other than that, she'll be back to her old self. We tried to drop her off at Mom-Mom Ella crib. But she wasn't having it; she didn't want Luke to leave her."

"Well, that should be expected. I hope she heals from all of this, and where's her stupid ass mama." I said with so much anger, and little mama started doing somersaults in my belly.

"Girl, calm ya ass down while my baby in your stomach, and she's in the hospital; she was in bad shape when we got there. I thank God that nothing happened to Joi. 'Cause Luke wouldn't be able to deal with that shit."

Cash's phone started ringing and he went out of the room to answer. I didn't think anything of it though 'cause I know what he does for a living. I just hope after this baby is born he sticks to his future plans.

Chapter Five

Cash

My phone ringing brought me out of my thoughts. I looked down at it and saw it was Nadia. She had been calling me all day to spend time with my son. But shit got crazy with Meia. Granted, we were happy to have Joi back, the way Meia was lying out on the floor in front of her daughter was some fucked up shit. Which is why that bitch ass nigga got two bullets through his head, and two in the chest.

"Yo, Nadia what's up ma?"

"Cash, you said you were going to spend time with the baby today. I was trying to bond with my daughter while she was still here. She's leaving in three days, and I've been so busy with the baby I haven't really had any time to show her some attention."

Hearing her say that had me pissed, but I needed to stay in her good graces. I needed her and Kyndall both to be on my good side. She wanted to be supermom all of a sudden. That shit was for the birds. I don't know who she thought that she was fooling.

"Nadia. I know what I said, and I'm sorry I got caught up ma. But I'll be there as soon as I'm done working." I didn't know how the hell I was going to keep this shit up with both of them not knowing, there was no way that I was going to lose Kyndall and I had just gotten her back. I also knew that I couldn't let Nadia find out about my daughter with Kyndall because she was going to flip.

I just stood there for a minute getting my thoughts together. In a way, I hoped that Kyndall was going back to Memphis because that would give me time to get this shit figured out. I looked down the hall and there was a female standing in the hall talking to the nurse that had just left out of Kyndall's room. It looked like Nadia but there would have been a reason for her to be here. I made my way down the hall, and when I was halfway there my suspicions were confirmed. It was her.

I made my way to where she was so that I could see what she was doing here. She had just called going off and it didn't look like she was where she should have been. I was happy that her back was to me because I didn't want her to know that I was here. I wanted to see what she was saying. I walked as close as I could and just stood there.

"So, has he been here all day?" she asked the nurse.

"Not up here. He just got here; you know I had to call you boo. The chick good and pregnant too, girl." The nurse told her.

I wish that I could see Nadia's face. I knew that she was probably looking crazy as hell. What she said next told me what type of female that she really was.

"This nigga got me all the way fucked up. If he thought that I was going to let them live happily ever after, then he's a fool. I only had this baby so that I can be financially set for the rest of my life. Now don't get it fucked up, I love my son with all my heart, but if he would have been by Dre, I wouldn't have kept him. Shit, I might as well let them be; either way, his ass is gone, pay me.

Ugh, bitch, I'm so mad I just knew that hoe was going to stay gone. She should have died with her last baby. I wish that bitch and her baby would just go away," she said.

What she didn't know was that I was going to take my baby and she could go on about her life. I stood there a while longer just to see what else they were going to say. The crazy thing was that neither one of them noticed me 'cause they were so into what they were talking about. I walked off once I heard all that I needed to hear. Once I was down the hall, I called my mom.

"Hey son," she answered.

"Is my baby there with you?"

"Yea, he's right here sleep. Nadia said that she was going to get the baby, but that was like an hour ago."

"Ok well, when she comes back don't let her in and don't give her my baby. She on some other shit ma," I explained. I knew that my mama was going to say something crazy but I didn't care. She knew that if I was telling her that it was for a reason.

"Cash, you know that I don't like getting in the middle of your mess. I just got to go over Gloria's house because I can't do that. If I'm not here I can't let her in," she said before hanging up in my face. I just laughed and walked back in the room. Kyn was half sleep, Luke was rocking Joi and Shawnee was laying on the small sofa sleep. I looked at Luke and he just shook his head.

"Hungry Daddy," Joi said.

Before Luke could reply, Shawnee lifted her head up, "Yea, we hungry Daddy." He just dropped his head. He for sure had his hands full. Hell, all Shawnee did was eat when she wasn't pregnant so I know that's all that she is going to do why she is.

"Come on," was all he said before getting up. Once they were gone, I sat there debating on if I should tell her about Nadia and the baby. I knew that it would hurt her, but I couldn't keep it from her. That would be the same shit that Keem did. Then I knew that soon as I left here, I was going to have to deal with this shit with Nadia. I knew that she was a snake but damn I didn't think that it was that bad. That meant that was the reason why she was with me from the beginning. I trusted her at one point and this whole time she was playing my ass.

"What you thinking about?" Kyndall asked, pulling me from my thoughts.

"A lot of shit baby. How are you feeling?" I asked, trying to get off the subject. I didn't want her to start questioning me.

"I guess I'm ok." When she said that, I knew that she was not going to let it go. I just couldn't lose her again. I knew on the same token that if she found out from someone else that she was going to flip. Just as I was getting ready to speak, her phone buzzed. She had this look on her face that I couldn't read. She was just holding the phone.

"Who that?" I asked. By that time there were tears rolling down her face. I got up to go by her and she held her hand up to stop me.

"Cash is there something that you need to tell me?" she asked. I had no idea who she could have been talking about. Then it hit me. That nurse must have gone in her record and gave Nadia her number.

"Look baby, that was what I was getting ready to tell you. Nadia and I have a son together. I wasn't keeping it from you, I promise," I pleaded. I needed her to know that I wasn't on no fuck shit. I looked in her eyes and damn near wanted to cry. You could see the pain in her eyes and that was too much for me. I just got up and walked out. I knew that she didn't want to talk to me right now. So, I decided to give her a moment alone.

Keem

I've been chilling out in Atlantic City which was an hour away from Camden. I had been trying to get my mind right, but the drugs had a nigga's mind gone. I thought for sure I would be dead by now, but I'm guessing they not worried about me right now. I was still trying to get in touch with Kyndall, but her phone had been disconnected. Nobody was fucking with me, so I didn't know whether I should show my face or just keep laying low.

"What's up baby, are you good?" The hooker that had been kicking it with me for a couple of weeks asked. I was running out of my savings, and I knew for sure I was going to need more money to keep hiding. Plus, I knew when the money was gone and I couldn't keep her high she was going to bounce.

"Nothing just trying to figure out some money moves, so I could keep paying your fine ass."

"As long as you keep giving me that big, cock you good. I just won't be able to lay around with you all day. I'll need to head out to make me some money, but when I'm finished, I'll come back here to chill with you." I didn't know what it was, but I was starting to feel like this chick was feeling me.

I needed to figure out a way to get to the city to see what all was going on. I really needed to find out if Cash owed me any money from when we used to work together. I needed to think of who I could get in touch with from the inside. I needed the one person that worked heavy with me in the pharmacy. Only one person came to mind and I didn't know if he would tell me anything. I figured what the hell; maybe I could offer him some money. I pulled my phone out and dialed Jonathan's number.

"Yo, who is this?" He answered on the second ring.

"It's Keem; remember you used to work with me for Cashmere Whitfield."

"Yeah…I remember; what's good with you bro?"

"I wanted to know if you still work for him, and if so would you wanna make some money?"

"Yeah…I'm still there, and I'm always down to make some extra money. As long as it's nothing that's going to get me killed."

"Well, as you know Cash and I are not on good terms. All I wanna know is if he and my wife are together. If so where they staying at. I really just wanna know what's been going on. I'm so out of the loop."

"Well, my nigga money talks and bullshit walks. Where could we meet up so you can run me my bread? Then I'll find out everything you wanna know. You have to make sure none of what I tell you leads back to me. I need my job and most important I don't wanna end up somewhere stinking 'cause I'm fucking with Cash and Luke."

"First of all, you'll be fine; they will never suspect you. If anything, they gone think it's a street nigga telling all they business. How about we meet up tomorrow? I'm in AC so we can meet up somewhere in the middle, so you won't have to drive too far."

"Alright, as soon as I hang up, I'll text you the amount and the address we can meet up. Bro, please don't play me either 'cause I don't have to do this shit. If you're wasting my time, you'll definitely regret it."

I looked at my phone and started to shake my head. Who this geek ass nigga thought he was calling his self-checking me? I chuckled and told him I'll chat with him tomorrow.

Chapter Six

Shawnee

A Week Later ….

This damn baby was getting the best of me. I was tired and lazy as hell. I knew that I had dresses that needed to be done but I had no energy. All Joi and I did was watch TV and eat. My baby girl was gaining weight just like I was and dared somebody to say something.

"So, you gone, lay in bed all day?" Luke asked as he walked in with two plates.

I had no idea what was on the plates, but I was hungry, so I didn't care. I sat up so that I could get the food that I knew had to have been for me. Luke sat on the chaise that was across from the bed. Soon as he opened the bag, I smelled the hot sauce from the wings and my baby started doing flips. They looked so good that my mouth was watering.

"Where mines," I pouted as I watched him take a bite from the steaming chicken wing.

"Aww shit, you thought this was for you," he laughed.

I didn't see shit funny. He knew that I was hungry. Before I knew it, I was crying. Joi was looking at me like I was crazy, and his ass was eating like he didn't care that I was hungry.

"Bruh, are you really over there crying?"

"You don't care that I'm hungry. You just gon' let me and my baby starve. You knew that we were hungry. Why you doing me like this," I cried. Y'all, I had real tears like somebody died.

"Owww, daddy you make mommy cry," Joi said as she rubbed my back like I always do her when she cried. Luke just shook his head and walked out of the room. He came back a few minutes later with three plates. I was smiling big as hell, but tears were still rolling. He handed me one of the plates, and I damn near dropped it trying to get it open.

There were three different kinds of wings. I had tears rolling but that didn't stop me from digging into the food that was in front of me.

He handed Joi hers and then he sat the other one in the middle of us. It was full of seasoned fries. I swear to you that I was in love. The fries and wings were crispy just like I liked them.

"You happy now?" I just nodded my head 'cause there was no way that I could talk. I was too busy stuffing my mouth. His phone rang so he answered on speaker.

"What's good," I heard Cash's voice come through the phone.

"Not shit, just got up; finna go get my lil nigga and then go check on Kyndall." Her doctor came here so that she wouldn't have to fly back to Memphis and so that we could keep an eye on her. Danni went back home yesterday. Kyndall didn't want to be here but she had no choice. She was heartbroken when she found out about Nadia's baby that she wouldn't talk to anyone other than me and Mom-Mom. She was even mad at Luke. Cash had been going up there every day, but she wouldn't say two words to his ass. The only reason that she was ok with him coming up there was 'cause he would bring food.

"Fool let me tell you about this crazy ass girl. I came into the house with me some wings. Shit, a nigga hungry. I sat down to eat, and this girl busted out crying. Joi and I were just sitting looking," he laughed again at my expense.

"So, she was crying because you didn't bring her no food?" Cash asked.

"Yes, bruh. Like real tears." He knows how I feel about chicken. Why would he play with my emotions like that?

"Don't do my sister like that nigga," Cash defended me. I knew that someone loved me. He walked out of the room, so I knew that they were going to talk business. Joi and I sat in the bed and ate while we watched *Frozen* for the millionth time. We had watched it so much that I knew the words. Since he was gone, I decided to call Kyn to see what she was doing. I knew that she would understand how I was feeling.

"Hey fat girl," I greeted her soon as she answered. She hated when I called her that, but I didn't care.

"What's up prego? What y'all doing?" she asked.

"Girl, nothing; eating some wings looking at *Frozen*." She got quiet as hell. "What's wrong with you?" I could have sworn that I heard her sniffing like she was crying.

"Cash hasn't fed me and I want some wings." I busted out laughing and so did Joi. Now I see why he was laughing; shit was dumb ass hell.

"Stop crying boo; you know that nigga not gone let you go without eating. Just call and tell him that you want wings," I advised her. She just held the phone. I knew that she was debating if she wanted to call him or not. Like I said before she hadn't been talking to him.

"Can you just bring me some?"

"Yea," I lied. I wasn't going anywhere. This shit was going to put me right to sleep. We talked for a while longer then we ended the call. I didn't feel like getting up, so I called Luke's phone. He was going to be mad, but I didn't care; he would get over it.

"What Shawn?"

"Come here please baby. I will make it worth your time later." I knew that would get his ass in here in no time. He was a sucker for this sloppy toppy.

"What's up baby," he asked as he walked in the room with the phone to his ear.

"You still talking to Cash?" He nodded. I reached my hand out for the phone. I didn't care if they were talking business. I had some shit to say. He handed me the phone, and I made sure to rub his hand like I was a creep.

"So, look, my bestie was crying because you haven't fed her today. What's up with that?" I asked. He was laughing hard as hell. I didn't see shit funny.

"Man… that girl didn't have to tell me that she was hungry. I have been just taking shit up there, so I don't have to hear that shit. I'm headed there now; what did she say what she wanted?"

"Wings," was all that I said before giving Luke the phone back. He grabbed his food and walked back out of the room. I knew Joi and I would be sleeping soon. She was already laying down. I got up so that I could throw the food boxes in the trash and damn near fell. I need to do better; my house was a mess and there was shit everywhere. As bad as I wanted to get back in the bed I didn't. I headed downstairs so that I could start cleaning my house.

Nadia

I had been calling Cash for almost a week and hadn't gotten an answer. I knew that he was probably mad because I sent his sweet little Kyndall that picture. She needed to know that I was first and would always be. He was just mad right now, but I knew that he would get over it. He would get tired of having CJ and call me.

"Bitch, I need to get high," my homegirl Karen said, pulling me from my thoughts.

"Shit, me too. Just wait for my sister to come get my daughter then we can go get something," I told her. Since I had been free from this little one, I had started some bad habits. I was popping pills and smoking bud again. I wanted to get high too, but I knew that if I did it around my daughter then she would go and tell Cash, or my sister and I couldn't have that. My sister said that she was on the way, so I was on the porch waiting. Just as I was getting ready to text her, she pulled up. I took my baby to the car and made sure that she was good before letting them pull off. Once they were gone, I called up my pill man. It took him no time to get here.

"Bitch, what are you doing?" I asked Karen.

"Breaking them down to powder. It gets you high fast and you stay high longer," she explained. I was looking at her crazy because I wanted to see how this shit worked. I watched as she broke the pill down and snorted it. That bitch looked like she was in heaven and I wanted to be the same way.

"Here do mines," I told her. She did as I asked. We laid back in the bed and let the high kick in. What she said was true. I was high as hell and ready to fuck. I looked over and apparently, she was horny as well because she was playing with her pussy. That shit turned me on so I sat up so that I could get a good view. Just as I was getting ready to start playing with mine someone knocked on my front door. She went to go answer since she is the one that was waiting on someone to pull up. She walked in with some fine ass nigga. He took a seat across the room in the chair. Soon as she laid back down, she started back playing with her pussy like he wasn't in the room.

He picked up the tray that she was using to break down the pills and did the same. I was slick amped because I knew that he was finna get us high.

"Go help her," he demanded. I was feelin' freaky, so I did as he told me. Before I knew it, I was eating her pussy like I had been doing that shit all my life. He handed me the tray and I took a line of the smashed pills. My high went up instantly. That must have been a different kind of pill. Karen took a line and before I knew it, we were full out fucking each other. He was just sitting back watching us while smoking a blunt. She must have seen me looking at him because she got up and pulled him over to the bed. He stripped out of his clothes in no time, so he can join the party.

****

The next morning, I woke up with a big ass headache, not really remembering what was goin' on. I remembered Karen and me getting high and fooling around, but I don't remember the dude that was lying in between us. The sound of my phone goin' off brought me out of my thoughts. I picked it up when I saw that it was Cash.

"Get that nigga up out ya crib. I was bringing the baby over to see you while I took care of some business." Hearing him say that had me shaking my head. If he only sees what I had laid up in here, he would kill me.

"Ok... can you give me an hour please. I need to shower and straighten up a little."

"Alright cool, and Nadia don't make me regret this. 'Cause to be honest I don't wanna bring him over. But my mama said I can't keep him away from his mother too long. So, know if you fuck up, I'll never let you see him again."

I didn't say shit. I just hung the phone up and started nudging Karen so she can get her and Mister Mystery Man up out of here.

"Come on, baby... I'm trying to sleep." Karen cooed while staring up at me.

"I'm sorry, boo, but y'all gotta go. Cash is coming to bring the baby over." The dude heard me say Cash and he jumped up.

"Cash who?" He asked with wide eyes.

"Cash is my baby's father. Why you say it like that?"

"Cause I only know of one Cash, and that nigga is running shit around here. Karen, why didn't you tell me she was Cash's girl."

"Nigga, 'cause she ain't Cash girl. She's just his baby mama. Let me find out you about to piss in ya pants or something." We both giggled.

"Bitch, fuck you, it ain't even nothing like that. Now, come on so we can get the fuck out of here." He snapped at Karen and she got her ass up really quick. After they both left, I hopped in the shower and took care of my hygiene. Once I was satisfied, I jumped out and threw on some tights and an oversized t-shirt. I then straightened up a little. I was happy to see that it was a couple of condoms on the floor, so I was happy I protected myself, 'cause only God knows what my hot ass did last night.

"Yo Nadia... Where you at?" Cash yelled up the steps.

"I'm coming down now," I yelled back.

I really need to get my key back from this nigga, but then again, he ain't having that since he pays all the bills.

"Hey, mama's suga bear!" I cooed while holding my arms out for my son. He looked just like his father and he made me sick.

"What's good yo? We need to talk really quick before I go."

"What now Cash? I said I was sorry for how I told Kyndall, but she needed to know. 'Cause you wouldn't have told her. You seem to always spare her feelings but fuck mine. I know you love her, and I'm cool with just co-parenting. I'm not gon' keep getting hurt by you." I said in one breath.

"Whatever Nadia... you didn't love me Ma. All you wanted was a meal ticket and you got it 'cause I ain't gone never see my son or his sister hungry. But we gon' do this shit together. I'mma take care of the utilities for six months, but after that, you have to figure it out. Of course, I'mma always make sure it's food here for Nya when she comes over. The house was paid for with cash money, so you really have nothing to keep up with but electric, gas, water, and cable if you want it. It's ya crib so I can't tell you who you can have in here. But don't be doing any bullshit in front of my son or Nya. I already heard you be on good bullshit already. So, make sure when my son here you chill out with that bullshit Nadia."

News sure does travel fast. How the fuck did he hear some shit about me already? I couldn't believe he was making me pay my own bills. I knew this shit wasn't coming from anybody but that fucking Kyndall.

"Is there any more rules and regulations daddy?" I asked sarcastically.

"Nadia, I'm serious, Ma, so cut the bullshit. You already know my attitude can get on ten real quick. Now fuck with me if you want to it's gone be a problem. I'll be back to get him tomorrow; if you need anything call me. If I don't answer, contact my mama."

That was the last thing Cash said before he walked out of the door. I had an attitude about all of this, but I couldn't dwell on it. I needed to figure out a way to get some money without goin' back to my old days.

Chapter Seven

Meia

A few days later…

"Noooo… Tory, please don't make me do it. Joi is in here."

"I don't give a fuck about that little bitch being in here.
You better do what the fuck I said and suck his dick."

"You know what man… I'm out of here. I didn't come here
for a couple's argument. I could be at the strip joint getting
my dick sucked."

"See what the fuck you did. You made the dude leave and
messed up my money."

Whap, Whap, Whap…

"How about I call on a couple of clients that like little
girls."

"Noooo… Tory please. I'll do whatever you want me to
do."

"Nope bitch, you too fucking late. You already made me
miss out on money."

"Over my dead body Tory. I will not let you harm my
daughter."

I woke up out of my sleep in a wet nightgown drenched
from sweat due to the nightmare I had just had. Luke had
helped me enroll in rehab right after I got released from the
hospital. I was shocked to see his face. I was for sure that
he was going to kill my ass, but instead, he talked to me
about getting help. He assured me that he was only doing it
'cause of Joi. He told me that she had been having
nightmares and asking was I alive. So, he had let me call
her the minute I woke up. I apologized to him about his
mama, and he just wouldn't listen to me. Shawnee told me
to give him some time. I was shocked when she called to
talk to me, but she told me that she and I would do all the
communication when it came to Joi. That's how mad Luke

still was. I apologized to him and his mama. I had to; that was a part of my recovery.

"Hey, I'm Ms. Terrance. I'm one of the counselors here. How have you been?"

"I'm ok Ms. Terance. Just tryin' to take it one day at a time."

"That's good. I'm here today to try and talk you into doing meetings with other women that have been in your shoes. It would help with your recovery. Talking about it always seems to work."

"I think I would be able to do that. I have to get me some clothes and other personal items. I came here with nothing and actually don't have any family that I deal with."

"Ok… well, you do me a favor and I'll do one for you. You promise me you'll make the meetings next week, and I'll be sure to have some clothes and personal items ready for you in a couple of days."

"Alright, you got a deal!" I assured Ms. Terrance right before shaking her hand. Once she got up and left, I laid across the bed trying to get my thoughts together. There was a knock at the door bringing me out of my thoughts. I jumped up and answered the door, and Shawnee walked in holding Joi's hand. She was beautiful and her baby bump was finally sitting out. She looked to be about five months.

"Mom-mom!" Joi screamed while jumping into my arms.

"Hey, baby! How are you? I miss you so much. What are you doing here?"

"When I woke up in the morning, I asked mama Shawnee can we see you, and her say yeah. So, we came." Joi rambled on.

"Awww… well, I'm glad you and mama Shawnee came. I was kind of bored here."

"So, what you been up to Meia?" Shawnee asked.

"Just taking it one day at a time, has been my new line. The counselor just left right before y'all came in; she wants me to start sessions with other women that went through or goin' through what I went through. I told her I would, but I don't have any clothing or personal products. She said she will get the things that I need."

"Why didn't you call us?" Shawnee asked.

"I couldn't call Luke. I'm his least favorite person right now."

"He's mad but Luke has a heart of gold; he would have handled this. Text me your size and I'll go get you some things when we leave up out of here."

Shawnee was such a lifesaver, and I didn't understand what made her wanna help me all of a sudden.

"Thank you! So much. I just don't know how I'm goin' to repay you for all you do for me."

"Get yourself together for the sake of Joi. That's all the thanks I need."

"How's mama doing?" I asked referring to Luke's mother.

"She's coming along really good. We got her doing therapy two times a day. They say she should be coming home after she does all her days of therapy." I was happy to hear that. Luke's mom had such a great soul. I hate that I caused her pain. Hell, she was the only person that was there for me when I didn't have shit.

"That's great." A part of me wanted to ask how Luke was doing but I didn't want to give her the wrong impression. I was more than grateful that he spared my life. He helped me get clean and that was more than I could ask for. The counselor would say that I did it myself, but they didn't know the half.

"Mommy look," Joi said, pulling my attention. She showed me the blocks that she had built. My baby was so pretty. It just broke my heart knowing that she would remember all the bad things that I did to her. Shawnee stepped out in the hall, so I took that time to tell my baby that I was sorry for all the bad that I had done.

Shawnee

I hate taking Joi to that place that Meia was in, but I know that she needs to see her mother. Every time we left, she would be quiet the whole way home. That was so weird to me. I knew that she needed to see her, but this was the last time that I'll be taking her.

"Can we get ice cream?" Joi asked from the back seat.

"We have some in the house, so you can get some after dinner. What do you want for dinner?" I asked. I just prayed that she didn't say Cheesecake Factory. I used to love that place but she had worn it out. Now I can't stand to eat that shit. The smell made my stomach hurt.

"Can you cook Chicken Mama Shawnee?" My baby knew that I would cook her anything that she wanted no questions asked.

"Yes, baby." We pulled in the driveway and there was a car there that I hadn't seen before. Luke didn't have people over often so a part of me wanted to call him to be cautious. Just as I was dialing his number, I saw him and Cash walk out with the guy that was at the hospital when we came back from Memphis. Soon as Luke saw me, he headed to the car. That alone put a smile on my face.

"How my two favorite ladies doing?" he asked as he opened the door for us at the same time.

"We are good daddy. Mommy cooking chicken. Is that my uncle Cash?" she asked all in one breath. She did give us time to answer before she ran off in the direction that Cash was in. We both just laughed. Soon as I got out the car, she rubbed my round belly. It seemed that I had gotten bigger overnight. I was so ready to get this baby out of me. Hell, most days I couldn't even get out the bed. Mom- Mom swore that I was having twins. He grabbed my purse and walked with me to the door. Joi and Cash were already in the house.

"Why are you looking at me like that?" I asked Luke; he just smirked and pulled me in for a kiss.

"Just admiring how fine my baby mama is. My baby got that ass looking fat," he joked. I just laughed because he was doing the most as always. One thing I can say was that he made sure that I knew how good I looked. Luke was the perfect man for me.

"How did the visit go?"

"It was ok. I'm going to get her some clothes and stuff. Joi enjoyed spending time with her. I can honestly say that I'm proud of her. She is really doing good. Maybe the next time you should take Joi," I recommended. He gave me a weird look but didn't reply. I wasn't worried about them doing anything or nothing like that. I knew that he didn't want her ass, especially after what she had done.

A few days ago, I had gotten a call from a client in Atlanta. I had created a dress for her a while back and she was looking to get another one done as well and a dress for her daughter's prom. I had been debating on telling him because I knew that he would have a fit if he knew that I was going to be gone. Since we had been together, I had been doing everything from home. I had a whole studio downstairs, but I knew that I was going to have to be there for this client because she was very picky. The last time that I did some work for her she stopped by every day. I just needed to figure out a way to tell him that I was going. It wasn't for another month, so I had time to figure it out.

"Joi wants chicken so what sides do you want?" I asked Luke.

"It doesn't matter baby; whatever you cook is good," he assured me. I just nodded and sat the chicken that I had just taken out into the sink. I really didn't feel like cooking, so I decided on green beans and diced potatoes. I knew that wouldn't take long.

As I made my way around the kitchen my mind went to Kyndall. My girl was going through it. Seemed that no matter how hard she tried to get her life in order she kept getting the bad end of things. I just wished that Cash would have told her about CJ. I also hate the way that Nadia told Kyn. She should have let Cash tell her, but we all knew that wasn't going to happen because she was childish as hell. She hated Kyndall so there was no way that she was going to let her be great. I just hope that the stress that she is going through doesn't hurt the baby.

"Baby, I need to take care of some shit. Joi is in her room looking at the TV."

"Ok baby. I love you. Be careful."

He kissed me and headed out the door. I decided to call Danni to check on her. She had gone back home and hadn't called.

"Hey boo," she answered.

"Hey, love. I was just checking on you. I hadn't talked to you since you been back home."

"I know girl. I been so busy. I'm coming back up there in a week or so. Kyndall swears that y'all don't love her. She so damn extra," Danni laughed. She wasn't lying either. Kyndall was dramatic as hell all of a sudden.

"Girl, she's crazy. Cash has been up there all day every day; she just not talking to him so that's why she is saying that," I advised Danni. She didn't know much about all what had happened with Nadia. Kyndall kept saying that she didn't want to talk about it.

"I just don't want her stressing the baby out. A part of me is happy that he found her but then the other side is mad she's going through this. I'm happy he can be there because she didn't need to go through this pregnancy alone. But if I would have known he came with all this extra stress that we were trying to keep her from, I would have rather he found out after she gave birth."

"True," was my only reply. I had been knowing Cash my whole life, so I knew that he meant good. He was one of the good guys. Danni and I talked until Joi came down to say that she was ready to get in the tub. I fed her then bathed her. She was in the bed and sleep by ten. That was a little later than what I prefer, but I was good with it for the day.

Luke was still gone so I decided to get in the tub and soak. It had been a while since I had done that. I was so damn big that I just took showers most of the time because I didn't want to get stuck. Soon as I sat down, I threw my head back. The water felt so good. I sat there for what seemed like forever. I refilled the tub twice. When my body felt good, I tried getting up and couldn't. I knew that Luke was going to make fun of me. I grabbed my phone and called him.

"What's up baby," he answered.

"Ummm… I'm stuck in the tub," I told him. He just burst out laughing.

"Yo, what I tell you about that shit. I'm on the way man," was all that he said before ending the call. Just as I was cutting the water back on Joi walked in. She scared the shit out of me.

"Mommy, I want Daddy," she said sitting down on the floor by the door where she always did when I was in the bathroom.

"He on the way baby." Thirty minutes later he walked in the bathroom. Joi was looking at YouTube on her iPad and I was reading. He pulled his phone out and took a picture. That shit pissed me off because I was looking a mess.

"Why would you do that Luke?" I said rolling my eyes. He was standing there laughing, and I was ready to get out this damn tub. I guess he saw that I was getting mad because he walked over and helped me.

"Make that yo last time doing this shit if I'm not home. What if something would have happened," he fussed as if he wasn't just laughing a second ago. My damn body was shriveled and looking pale as hell. He picked Joi up and walked out of the room. I dried off and got dressed so that I could go and fix his food. When I made it downstairs, he and Joi were on the couch looking at *Finding Nemo*. I was so over that damn movie; that's all we had been watching. I headed to the kitchen so that I could fix their plates. Once I was done, they paused the movie and came to the kitchen. We all sat at the table and listened to Joi tell us what she wanted for Christmas. That little girl was so damn spoiled. I knew that whatever we didn't get Cash and Kyndall were going to get it.

Chapter Eight

Nadia

It had been three damn days since Cash dropped CJ off. He had never left him with me this long since he had been born unless he was with Kyndall. She was all his ass thought about. She should have been the last thing on his mind seeing that she was married to his ex-best friend. Just as I was laying CJ in his bed my phone rang. I saw that Karen was calling. I hadn't really talked to her because I knew that she would want to get high and I couldn't do that if CJ was here. That was part of the reason that I was ready for his daddy to come and get him.

"What's good boo?" I answered.

"Shit girl, calling to see if you wanted to get out tonight?" I knew that she was going to ask that. I wanted to tell her yes so bad, but I knew that wasn't going to happen unless my baby was gone. See, she had kids but they lived with their father. My baby was here with me. Hell, she was one of the parents that left her kids at home alone and they were only three and five. I knew for sure Cash would kill my ass.

"I have to see. CJ dad still hasn't come back to get him. You know that other hoe pregnant, so he's been tending to her," I admitted. That shit really had me hot because he was never like that with me. His ass would go weeks without calling or coming by.

"Girl, you better than me. I would drop his ass off right where his ass was at. He would have me fucked up," she added. I had thought about that. A part of me wanted to do that but I didn't want to have to deal with Cash. He was nice but when it came to CJ, he was a whole other person. She didn't know Cash like that. He would kill her ass and me.

"Cash would kill me. I'm going to call him. I'mma call you back after I talk to him," I told her. After I ended the call with her, I called Cash but he didn't answer. I called his mom but didn't get an answer from her either. Since I couldn't catch up with them, I decided that I would clean my house. I knew that it wouldn't take long because I made sure that I kept it clean because Cash was picky when it came to CJ.

Once I was done, I pulled my phone out and decided that I would call Cash once more, and just like I thought, he didn't answer. I was pissed the fuck off, but I wasn't goin' to dwell on it. I decided to scroll my Instagram and a picture of Shawnee and Luke popped up; he was kneeled down, placing a kiss on her stomach. The shit angered me to the point a couple of tears dropped. Why couldn't I find someone to love me like this? Shit was straight until little miss goody two shoes came back to town.

I jumped up off my couch and headed to my room to throw some clothes on. Since Cash didn't wanna come to get his son, why not just drop him off at the hospital with his stepmama. They had everything he needed there. Shit, why must I be stuck with CJ all these days while they chill like the perfect couple.

Kyndall

"What girl?" Shawnee answered. I knew that she was going to answer like that. I had been calling her all day. I wasn't talking to Cash, so I needed someone to talk to and she knew that.

"Nothing, how long will it before you come back?" I asked. I was being a baby, but I didn't care. She said today that she would be here as soon as she was done with what she was doing. I ended the call and then called Mom-Mom. I knew that she was going to answer for me. Just as I was getting ready to call her, Cash walked in the room. I just rolled my eyes. He was always here. I guess he thought that would make me talk to him, but it wouldn't. I was done; all that we had to talk about was this baby that we were about to have together.

"So, you really gon' keep acting like this?" Cash asked me as he made his way to the side of the bed.

My heart started beating fast as hell. When he made it to me, he kissed me, and I damn near forgot why I was mad. His kiss was so soft. I accidentally let out a moan. He smirked and walked back to the bag that he had set down before coming over to me. I knew that it was some food because if he didn't do anything, he made sure that I was well fed.

"Has the doctor been in here today?" he asked. I didn't want to reply but I decided that was the least that I can do.

"Nah, I'm waiting now. I'm ready to go home," I damn near whined. I was so ready to go. I had been in this hospital too long for my liking. I prayed that I would be going home because I wanted to lay in a real bed.

"Ok, I'm finna go and see what's up," he said before walking out the room. I dug into my food and was done in no time. I had to use the restroom so I adjusted myself so that I could get up just as the door to my room opened. I turned around and saw Nadia. I just rolled my eyes and got up.

"Why are you here?" I asked.

"I just wanted to drop my son off so that he could spend some time with his father." She had this look in her face when she looked at my stomach, so I decided to just sit back down on the bed. That way, I knew that the chances of her doing something stupid was slim. If I would have walked past, a part of me knew that she would push me down or something. I couldn't take that chance. There was no way that I would survive losing another baby.

"Well, his father is down the hall; you should go and find him."

"You know, Kyndall, we have so much in common. I mean, shit, we even like the same niggas," she laughed.

"You don't have to look like that. Our kids are going to be siblings, so we need to get along. I shared the dick with you but I'm not sharing him, so you need to get that in your head. I will make sure that your baby is good when it's with me," she laughed.

She had to have been on drugs or something to think that I would have my baby around her. Hell, if I found out that he had my baby around her I was going to kill his ass. I just wish that he would have just left me alone. I was doing good; my baby was doing good. Now I'm stuck in this damn hospital looking crazy.

"Can you leave," was all that I had to say. I was done with all of this including Cash. I didn't need this stress.

She sat that baby carrier down and walked out the door. I was in shock. Like, this girl really left her baby here. Who does that? I sat there for a minute making sure that she was gone then I got up and got the baby. He was laying there knocked out. He was so handsome. When I picked him up, his diaper was soaked. That's when I noticed that he didn't have a baby bag. I shook my head because this was the woman that he was going to marry. I buzzed the nurse station and asked her to come down. Her and Cash rushed in at the same time. That meant that he was down there with them. Right after they came in so did the doctor.

"Hey, hun can you get a few diapers and some wipes?" I asked the nurse. She didn't ask any questions; she just walked out of the room. Cash was still standing there as if he was trying to figure out what was going on.

"Hey, Kyndall. How are you feeling today," Dr. Chin asked? That was my doctor from Memphis. She had flown down just to come and check on me.

"Ok, I guess. I got a headache. Wishing that I was home." I said as I admired the baby that I was holding. Cash made his way over to me. He reached for the baby, but I didn't want to let him go. I was stuck on the fact that this little baby looked just like him. I was amazed.

"Let me check your blood pressure," Dr. Chin requested. I switched the baby to my other arm and held my arm out so that he could take my blood pressure. I hated the blood pressure cups because they made my arm hurt. Just as the doctor was finishing, the nurse walked back in with a cart full of stuff. I knew that I wasn't going to need all of it but I didn't complain. "Your blood pressure is a little high so make sure that you are staying calm. Since you are eight months, we are going to take the stitches out. Meaning that she could come at any time. I know that you want to go home, but I think that it will be best for you to stay here. I don't want you to get home and have any complications. Dad makes sure that you keep mommy stress free. The smallest thing can harm the baby. And speaking of a baby, who is this handsome guy," she said, taking the baby from my hand.

"That's my son CJ," Cash said. Dr. Chin looked at him with the side-eye and handed him back to me.

I laid him down so that I could change him. The nurse had even given me clean onesies. His mama was so sad. There is no way that my baby would be looking like this. Hell, I can't believe Cash is going for this shit. We talked with the doctor for a few more minutes then she left. Once she was gone, I looked to Cash. He had this look on his face that I knew all too well. He was going to hurt her ass.

Chapter Nine

Luke

A Week Later…

I had been sitting in my car at the warehouse waiting for Cash's slow ass for an hour. That was the only nigga that I knew that was late for everything. I don't care what we were doing or where we had to be, he was going to be late no question. I didn't complain because sitting here gave me a chance to watch what these niggas had going on. I had seen a few things that needed to be addressed.

"Yo, bro what's good with you. Sorry, I took so long. I was talking to Chip. He was telling me about this new vacation spot he got out in the Poconos. He told me we can stay there free of charge anytime we ready. I told him maybe in three weeks. I'mma try to give Kyn some time to have the baby."

"That's what's up; maybe we can do a family holiday vacation. Damn man… I'mma have to see if Shawn, ok with flying. If so, we gon' have to go ahead and take that trip. Shit, we can definitely use it. Did he say we can stay as long as we want?"

"Yup, it's all ours for as long as we want. I like that holiday idea. Maybe it'll snow, and we can have a great time." Cash beamed.

"Well, let me check with mama and Shawn and see if they're down. What about ya mama and pops?"

"They would love it as well. I wish we could get the place all decorated for Christmas before we even get down there."

"You can just get Chip to hook it up for us," I assured Cash.

"I'll hit him up tomorrow. After we make sure everyone is down to go."

"What about Keys? Is he gon' go with us or just handle shit here while we are gone?"

"He can stay here and run everything while we're gone. I talked to him about it already and he all for it. Plus, Kyn ain't gone be feeling his girl, and I know he ain't leaving her home."

"Good 'cause he's the only one I trust to make shit happen," I told Cash.

"What you gon' do about CJ though? Do you think Nadia is going to give you a hard time?"

"No… that bitch been tweaking lately. I think she's on something, so I've been thinking about taking him from her. But I have to talk to Kyn about it. I don't want to bring any more stress on her so I'mma wait until she gives birth to my seed."

"Damn…shits crazy; you know why she is doing that though. I told you to spare her life in case the baby was yours, but you took it too far and moved her in giving her hopes that you knew weren't going down. You had her thinking Y'all were going to be one happy family then when Kyn got back down here. You gave her ya ass to kiss. I know you love your junior, but how you did Nadia was fucked up bro for real. I know she did you dirty, too, but you already knew she was a hoe and you continued to still smash." I admitted.

I knew he didn't like what I was saying but I didn't give a damn. He should have taken her ass home as soon as he let her live. But no, he wanted to lock her up and she started to get feelings again. He brought all this shit on himself, and he better hope Kyn brings that baby into this world healthy with no complications. Because if she doesn't, the first thing that's going to happen is everyone is going to blame it on him.

"Man…I know I fucked up. I'm trying to get my shit together. I love Kyndall and I pray that she brings my baby into this world healthy and safe. So, we can move on with our lives. I promise never to do anything to ever hurt her again. From now on, I'm making sure to put everything on the table."

"Good because she's been through a lot and she deserves to finally have happiness. Keep your thoughts about getting CJ until after the baby is born. Since we are going on the family vacation we might as well enjoy our holiday?"

"Yeah, that's a good idea. I'm not gone tell Kyn just yet. I'mma wait until she has the baby. They've been monitoring her pressure and it's been ok. Nothing has been bothering her lately, and I'm thankful. I thought the day Nadia dropped CJ off at the hospital it was going to make her lose it. But she was so, loving and caring to my son."

"Well, you already know how Kyn is. I wouldn't have seen it any other way. You see how she is with Joi and she's been that way ever since you introduced us."

"Yeah, you're right. So, where are we headed to?" Cash asked right before his phone chimed.

The look in his eyes and the way he hit his fist on the dashboard told me he was pissed. He hung the phone up and told me to head to his mama's crib.

"What the fuck happened bro?"

Nadia's simple ass dropped the baby off to my mama's crib and he was shitty and wet. My mama said he has a bad diaper rash. When she dropped him off at the hospital last week, he was wet as shit, and the bitch didn't bring a diaper bag. Kyn had to call and get shit from the hospital."

"Yeah, that bitch out of pocket." I snapped while speeding up my pace.

I pulled up to Cash's parent's crib in ten minutes. We both jumped out of the car and headed inside.

"Mama where you at?"

"I'm in the living room. I'mma tell you this one time and one time only. When I get a hold of that skank, I'm beating her trifling ass. This is getting out of hand; you need to figure out how you gon' get my grandbaby. I tried working with her and giving her the benefit of the doubt, but she's showing her true colors. That's probably why she doesn't have that little girl." Mama went on and on.

"Ok… Mama I'mma get it together. I promise you."

"You better Cashmere, and I mean it. Hey Luke. How are you baby? Where's my princess at?"

"Hey, Mama… she's home with Shawnee probably eating everything in the damn house." I chuckled.

"Leave my babies alone. Let them have whatever they want. They are eating for two. You make sure you bring them both over to see me soon. I'm thinking about giving Kyndall a big baby shower the day she's released from the hospital. So, make sure you tell Shawnee to come to see me and bring Mom-Mom Ella over here."

"Ok… mama I got you as soon as I get home."

"Well, when were you gone tell me about all of this." Cash sucked his teeth.

"When you got here, but now I'm pissed and don't really wanna talk to you. I swear I thought I told you when you were younger watch where you are slinging dick. Who you have kids by means something? I hope you don' with this hoe. You need to put a ring on Kyndall and sit ya fast ass down somewhere."

I never heard mama talk like this before. I just stood on the side laughing my ass off. I knew Cash was pissed at her last statement. I feel where she was coming from, though, but who was I to judge? Look who I had a daughter by. I don't regret Joi at all, but I wish I would have second guessed dealing with Meia's simple ass. My phone ringing brought me out of my thoughts. I looked at it and saw it was Shawnee.

"Hey, beautiful… what's up?"

"Baby… are you with Cash? I called his phone twice and he didn't answer."

"Yeah, he's right here; what's wrong?"

"They can't get Kyndall's pressure down and they may have to take the baby out."

"Ok… we will be right there. Come on, bro; it's Kyn; we gotta get to the hospital."

After we told mama what was going on, we hurried out of the door. I could tell that Cash had a worried look on his face. But I was sure everything was going to be just fine.

Cash

Luke and I were just now making it into the hospital. I already had a band on, so I ran straight up to the labor and delivery floor. By the time I got to the room they already had Kyndall in the back, and Shawnie was standing in the hallway crying.

"What's wrong sis? Where is she?"

"They had to hurry and take her back. To do an emergency c-section. Go let the nurse know you're the daddy and see if you can go to the back; hurry up." Shawnie said in an anxious tone.

I hurried and did as she said.

The doctors helped me put the gown and everything on then they took me right back. They talked me through what was going on, and they said everything was fine with the baby, and they were finally able to get Kyn's pressure stable.

When I made it to the back, the doctors directed me to stand at the top of the bed where Kyndall's head was. They had me behind a screen that separated me from the sterile area, where they were doing the c-section. I thought to myself good cause I didn't think I could see that shit. I did wanna see when the baby came out, so I asked the doctor, was there a way for me to see. She told me yes and placed a mirror next to me.

It seemed like forever when they finally were pulling my baby out. An hour later, Kyndall and I were blessed with a healthy baby girl. The doctors took her to clean her up and get her measurements. Being as though Kyndall had been through so much to have a baby, she needed to see that everything was alright. Of course, she was still drowsy, but I was able to hold the baby close to her face so she could see her. The tears that formed in her eyes told me that she was the happiest she had been in a long time.

"Alright, dad… we're going to move the baby to the nursery, so we can tie mom's tubes then close her up. Do you have any questions before the nurse walks you out?" I wanted to say something about the tie tubes part, but I left it alone. I knew Kyn had been through far too much to be even thinking about having any more kids.

"No…just show me where my baby is going to be and come get me when you're done with my future wife," I said to the doctor causing her to smile at me.

"Ok…once you get to the nursery, they should be able to tell you her weight and size. Then when Mrs. Richardson is back in her room and comfortable, we will let you know.

****

Kyndall was finally up and all of our family was in attendance. Cassidy Heaven Whitfield had stolen everyone's heart just that fast. Baby girl weighed seven pounds, four ounces and she was twenty-one inches long. She was spitting image of me just like CJ was; it was safe to say their mamas hated me when they were pregnant.

"Baby, she is so beautiful." My mama said while pulling me in for a hug. She just hated my guts earlier, but now she loves me. I started to think she only cares about her grandbabies, to hell with me."

"Thank you, mama, she is isn't she?"

"Both my grandbabies are. Thank you so much for giving me them." She cooed while kissing CJ on his cheeks.

I had so many people here I had to ask them for a big room, and of course, I would be staying here until they released her. My mama, Shawnie, Danni, Mom Mom, and Luke's mama was getting the shower together since Kyndall had to stay for another 4-5 days. They wanted to make sure her pressure was managed before she left.

There was a knock at the door and in walked Keys and his girl. Kyndall's face was torn up, but I gave her a look begging for her to chill out. I knew Chrissy used to deal with Keem, but she also went through some bullshit with

Keem that she didn't deserve. Kyndall looked at me, rolled
her eyes, but she kept it cordial. They both were holding
bags and Keys had flowers. I told him he didn't have to get
anything, but his hard-headed ass did anyway.

All my loved ones were here and today was yet another
happy day for me. Who would have ever thought that I
would have babies months apart? The shit was crazy, but I
would love them both the same until my casket dropped
and I meant that shit.

Chapter Ten

Chrissy

When Keys said that we were going to the hospital so that he could congratulate his boss on his new baby, I didn't expect for it to be Kyndall and Cash. I wanted to run but I knew that at some point I was going to have to face Kyndall. What better time than now?

"What's up y'all?" He said handing Kyndall the flowers that were in his hand and sitting the bags next to her. I wanted to say something to her, but I could tell by the look on her face that she was not fucking with me. Keys looked at me but didn't say anything. I guess he saw the look that she gave me. I knew that he was going to have something to say once we left.

"We good, man; just happy that baby girl is here," Cash said to Keys. He didn't even look my way. I knew that he didn't like me. I pray that he didn't get in Keys' ears about me because I had changed. I knew that no one trusted me, but I was trying to do better. I love Keys so I wasn't going to do anything to make him think otherwise.

I can't lie. A part of me envied Kyndall. After everything, she had the man that she wanted. I mean, I had my man but all in all I wanted Keem. Keys was good to me; he just didn't make me feel like Keem did. I just stood to the side and watched them interact.

"Can I see the baby?" I took a chance at asking. Kyndall gave me the nastiest look. I took that as a no, so I just pulled my phone out. It had been a minute since I had logged in Facebook, so I decided to do that. I felt so damn out of place. I was ready to go. I went straight to my inbox so that I could see who had been messaging me. I smiled when I saw that my homegirl Reecey from high school had hit me up. See, I keep my page active. I just didn't have it logged in on my phone. I replied to her and she messaged me back instantly. We went on and exchanged numbers before I logged out. When I looked up, Keys was standing over me. I'm happy that I wasn't saying any shit that I didn't have no business saying or talking to a nigga. I had tuned they asses out.

"Damn, you don't smile like that for me. Let a nigga find out you on some other shit," he said as he sat down next to me.

"You know you have to watch hoe's that tend to do the unthinkable," Kyndall said. As much as I wanted to say something back, I knew the best thing would be for me to keep my mouth shut.

"Baby, stay out them folk shit. Stay in yo lane," Cash said, causing her to roll her eyes.

She didn't say anything back; she just focused on her baby. I couldn't see her but I knew that she was probably so beautiful. Seeing her nurture her baby made me think about my baby. If I could go back I would change so much.

"How you end up with her?" Kyndall asked, pulling me from my thoughts. I wanted to say something so bad, but I knew that it would be a waste of time. What I did to her was wrong. I should have known that she wasn't going to be all buddy-buddy with me.

Keys looked at me and smiled causing me to smile. "It was kind of like you and Cash. I knew that I loved her when we were kids. She just never gave a nigga play."

Hearing him say that he loved me made my heart flutter. I knew that he loved me but it was something about when he expressed it to someone else that did something to me. I never would have thought that I would love this man the way that I do.

I looked at Kyndall and she was looking at her baby but I knew that she had heard him. The crazy thing is that she mad at me but she just had a baby by her husband's best friend. Shit, in my eyes, she is no better than me. We stayed for a while longer then headed home. The walk to the car was quiet, but soon as we got in Keys attacked me with kisses. That was one thing that I loved; he didn't mind showing me affection. Lucky for me I was wearing a dress. I pulled it up just as fast as he pulled me into the back seat. We were in the parking garage fucking like we were at home.

Kyndall

"Yo, you mean as hell," Cash said soon as Keys and his hoe left. I just shrugged and focused my attention on my baby girl. She was so damn beautiful. It was unbelievable that I birthed her. After so many tries I had finally brought a child into this world; it was more than I could ever ask for. I was a mother. I was going to spend my life making sure that she would be taken care of.

I looked over at Cash and he was smiling big as hell. I smiled back but it was more so because I thought about the fact that just yesterday I wasn't talking to him. A part of me was still mad but he had given me something that no one else had.

"I was just telling it how it is," I told him as I handed him Cass. The nurse was walking in to check my pressure. I prayed that it was down because I wanted to go home. I was doing my best to not stress.

"Ok, Kyndall looks like your pressure is doing good. We are going to keep you here for another day or so." I was happy as hell to hear that. I was more than ready to go. I wanted to sleep in a real bed. Once she was done, I laid the bed back so that I could try and get some rest.

"You hungry?" Cash asks as he places Cass in her bed.

"Naw, I'm good. I'm going to take a nap, while she sleeping," I said as I got as comfortable as I could.

"Ok baby. I'm going to go and check on CJ and pick up what you ordered from Target. I will be back after that. Call me and let me know if you need me," he said kissing me then Cassidy. I just nodded because I was waiting for the butterflies that were flying around in my stomach to settle. No matter how mad I was I knew that there was no way that I wanted to be without him. The crazy thing is that it took me so long to figure it out.

*****

It was finally time for me to go home. I was happy as hell. I had been sitting on the edge of this bed for an hour waiting on Cash ass to come and get me. Hell, I didn't get why I couldn't drive myself home; I wasn't disabled. I picked my phone up and snapped a picture for my baby just as her father walked in the door. He snapped a picture of me and her as I was snapping one of her. The nurse walked in as he was making his way to me.

"Hey, can you snap this pic for me?" Cash asked her. She agreed just as she was sitting the papers that were in her hand down. Cash pulled me close to him and kissed me on the neck, sending chills through my body. She snapped a few more pictures before handing Cash his phone back. She explained my discharge paperwork then we headed out.

Cash was so gentle. He made sure that Cass was in good. Like this nigga checked the seatbelt like five damn times. Then he helped me in the car. I wanted to sit in the back with her so he made sure that I was buckled in and we headed home.

I was so busy looking at my baby that I didn't notice that we were pulling up to a house that I hadn't ever seen. It was huge and beautiful. It looked like it should have been on the cover of a magazine.

"Who's house is this?" I asked as I climbed out soon as he stopped. I was in awe. Like, the driveway was even nice. I looked at him and he was getting Cassidy out the car like I didn't just asked him a question. He grabbed my hand and walked me to the door. When the door opened, I swear to you I could have died. Everyone that I loved was here. There was a huge banner that said 'Welcome home Cassidy'. There were people here that I hadn't seen in years. I was getting ready to make my way around the room then Shawnee pulled me off down this long hallway.

When we made it to the last door in the hall, she opened it and there was a full glam team there. I was so overwhelmed.

"Look, bitch you need to stop that damn crying so they can do your makeup," Shawnee fussed. I just rolled my eyes because she was acting like this was nothing. I didn't expect a baby shower. Hell, my ass had bought so much shit that I didn't know if itt all was going to fit in my little ass house.

I did as I was told so that I could get my makeup done. It didn't take her long to finish. Then the stylist came and straightened my hair. Once all of that was done, I sat there waiting on Shawnee to come back with my dress. I was excited because she had made me a dress. I was just hoping that I could fit it.

"Took you long enough," I said as she came in the door. She didn't reply; she just took the dress out of the bag. It was beautiful. It was a soft pink with a long train. She helped me into the dress. It fit me perfectly. When I looked at myself in the mirror I wanted to cry.

"Girl, please. Save those tears," Shawnee said as she adjusted my dress to make sure that it was perfect.

"Thanks, Shawnee," I said hugging her.

"You know I got you; now come on so we can go and party," she said, grabbing my hand and leading the way. When we made it back to the living area, Mom-Mom was holding Cassidy. I made my way over so that I could check on her. I knew that she was in a room full of people that loved her, but she was still my baby.

"Yes, mommy baby," I cooed. Cash was standing there looking good as hell. He was dressed in all white with a pink button up. He had dressed Cassidy in the cutest pink dress and CJ was dressed just like him. I walked over and kissed CJ just as Joi noticed that I was in the room.

"Tee Tee Kyn," she yelled causing everyone to laugh.

"Hey Joi," I bent down to kiss her. She hugged me so tight. I made my way around the room speaking to everyone. By the time I was done my feet were killing me. I took a seat and Cash rushed over to me.

"Baby you ok?" he asked. He had a worried look on his face that caused me to laugh.

"Yes Cash. My feet just hurting." He grabbed my feet and slid my shoes off. That shit felt good. But I couldn't help but be uncomfortable because he was rubbing my feet in a room full of people.

"Hold on, I got you some slides over here," he walked off and came back with a pair of Gucci slides. Once I had them on, he helped me up so that we could go and get something to eat. I was hungry as hell. I had my plate packed like my ass was still pregnant.

"Hey, I was wondering if we could talk," I heard someone say from behind me. I turned around to see Chrissy standing there looking stupid.

"What is it? Can't you see that I'm trying to eat," I said. She was ruining my mood. I don't know what she was thinking. Hell, who even invited her ass. They knew that I didn't fuck with her. Keys was cool but he needed to keep his hoe away from me.

"I know that you don't like me, but Keys works for Cash. We will have to be around each other at some point," she said as if that was going to change how I felt about her.

"Let me explain something to you. I…. DONT…. FUCK…. WITH …. YOU. You fucked my husband. You got pregnant; that is a no, no. The only reason that I'm having a conversation with you right now is because I don't want to ruin my baby shower. You can't be trusted. So, keep your distance for me," I told her before looking back down at my plate. I could feel her still standing there. I looked up and she had tears running down her face.

"I'm sorry for what I did. I know that it was wrong. I just hope that you can forgive me. I will sit your gift on the table and leave," was all she said before walking off. I could feel someone looking at me, so I looked up and Cash was watching me like a hawk. That meant that he sent her over here. Just as I was about to get up, Mom- Mom came and sat next to me.

"Why did you dismiss that girl like that," she asked. I wanted to roll my eyes so damn bad, but I knew that she would get in my ass. I was not about to get embarrassed. "What are you talking about?" Now I knew then that she was the one that sent her over here to talk to me.

"Little girl don't play with me. You need to let that pain go. You are way too blessed to be holding on to hurt. Trust me from what I've heard she has had her karma. I'm not saying that y'all have to be best friends, but you can be cordial with her."

Why was everyone so dead set on me talking to the woman that fucked my ex-husband? I was good on her ass. I wanted her to stay the fuck from around me. I didn't want anyone in my circle that I couldn't trust. Point blank. But I also knew that Mom-Mom wasn't going to let the shit go. She was going to talk about it every day until I gave in.

"Ok," was all that I said. I wasn't making promises. Once Mom-Mom walked off I finished my food and watched as Cash held our baby looking good as hell. I would have never thought that my life would be like this. As bad as I wanted to be mad at Cash I couldn't. I loved him. I just hate that I had to go through what I did to see that. I looked around the room and everyone was happy and having fun. That was all that I could ask for.

Chapter Eleven

Nadia

It had been a few weeks and I had been doing nothing but getting high out of my mind. Every time Cash tried to bring CJ over, I told him I was sick. I had seen pictures of the big ass house that he had brought Kyndall. I heard it was a push gift. The nigga had the nerve to give her a big ass baby shower as well. Seeing the pictures of her, him, their baby girl, and my son upset me so bad. Like, they were one big happy family, and I was sitting around here lonely and sad.

My sister had been calling me like crazy to keep Nya. Baby girl kept asking to come over to see CJ, and I kept telling her I was busy. But today I decided I was goin' to keep her and CJ for the weekend. At first, Cash was acting funny about it but he changed his mind when I told him that Nya wanted to see her brother.

"What you in here doing?" Cash asked, scaring the hell out of me. I didn't even hear him walk in.

"Nothing…just waiting on my sister to bring Nya. What's been up with you? How's Cassidy doing?"

"I'm good and she's doing well, growing fast."

"Why didn't you tell me you were moving? I know we're not together, but I think I got the right to know."

"Nadia…don't start cause I'm not in the mood for your shit. I drop CJ off and pick him up all the time. You have no reason to know where I lay my head. Plus, I don't need you doing pop-ups when you're in your feelings."

"You worried about me doing pop-ups, but you do them all the time. Shit, you let ya self in my house every time you come here, which I feel like it's disrespectful. Since you not my dude. What if I have company, and you just let ya self in."

"I always call before I come ma. I never just pop up over here, unless you don't answer when I call."

"That's what I'm saying. I might not wanna be bothered. So, maybe that's why I'm not answering."

"When you have a child ya ass supposed to pick up at all times Nadia. You know damn well I ain't calling you for shit unless it's for the baby. If you don't wanna be bothered, and you wanna continue to be a bitter bitch why don't you just give me full custody of my fuckin' son?"

"Cash, I'm not giving you my son, so you and that hoe can be one complete rich man's family. Go make ya own fuckin' son with her. Oh, I forgot, that bitch's eggs are rotten. She can't make no more babies."

The look he gave me showed me that he wanted to kill me, but I knew he wouldn't do shit in front of CJ which is why I jumped bad. The knock at the door brought us out of our stare down. I knew it was my sister, so I ran to answer it.

"Hey, Cashy!" Nya yelled and ran straight to him. I hated how she loved him so much.

"Hey, baby girl! How you been?" He beamed while picking her up and kissing her forehead.

"I ok...I wanna hold my bruda." Nya cooed.

"Alright...come on, let's wash ya hands, then I'll help you hold him." Cash assured her.

I let them do their thing while my sister and I headed to the kitchen to talk. I could tell by the way she was looking at me that she had something on her mind.

"What's up, sis? I can tell you wanna talk about something. So, talk to me."

"Nadia...I thought when you had CJ you were goin' to get yourself together?"

"What are you talking about?"

"Cash told me all the shit that has been goin' on around here. Thank God if something goes wrong CJ has a good father 'cause I wouldn't be able to take him too. I don't know when you're goin' to open your eyes and realize that you're not only living for you anymore. You have these beautiful kids. I'm not gone keep talking. I'mma let you go, but I hope you get your mind together."

I was so fucking pissed that these two were sitting and having a whole fucking conversation about me. Cash knew he was wrong for that. I'mma say something to him, but not right now. I'll say something when he comes to pick CJ up. My sister had left, and Cash was about to go as well until Nya started crying. She wanted him to watch a movie with him. One thing about Cash he couldn't tell her no, so he sat down and put the *Troll* movie on. An hour had gone by and just that quick him and Nya both were sleeping. The sight of both my kids lying on him sleeping was so priceless. I had to snap the pick and post it on Instagram. I had to get petty though the caption read.

 Nadia_hislove *Nights like this are always precious*@Cashdaman.

I had to tag his simple ass in it. I knew if he took too long to come home his bitch would be checking his social media, and that definitely would piss her off. I knew I was being childish, but I didn't give a damn. I hurried and eased CJ off of him in case he started to cry. I didn't want him to wake up. I was goin' to leave him there sleep. A half hour went by and Nya had climbed off the couch and came to climb in the bed with me. I went downstairs and Cash was still sound asleep. He didn't usually sleep this hard. I guess two small babies was keeping his ass up at night. I stood and stared at him for a minute and smiled then I made my way back upstairs.

"Nadia…wake ya crazy ass up." Cash barked causing me to jump out of my sleep.

"Why the fuck are you yelling like that?"

"Why didn't you wake me the fuck up? You know I don't be staying the fuck over here."

"You were resting so peacefully, and I didn't wanna bother you. Shit, you fell asleep chilling with the kids. Shit, it ain't

like you ain't never stayed out all night on your girl. You a
street nigga; she should already know what it is."
"I swear you stay on real bullshit, and if it wasn't for the
kids being here, I would beat ya ass." Cash snapped right
before he stormed out of the door.

Cash

I swear if it wasn't for the kids, I would have strangled this bitch. Kyndall had been calling me all fucking night. Then she had screenshotted a pic from Instagram that Nadia had posted and tagged me in. I was pissed like a mutha fucka 'cause I knew this shit looked all bad. But this time I really wasn't doing shit. I pulled out my phone so I could hit Luke up.

"Yo, bro what's good with you?"

"Man, I fucked up big time?"

"What happened?"

"I didn't stay home last night, but I wasn't on no bullshit. Let me explain before you start going off."

"Well, nigga go ahead and explain."

"I went over to drop CJ off last night, and Nya came. When I was about to leave, she cried for me to stay and watch *Trolls* with her. My dumb ass fell asleep and Nadia's dumb ass didn't wake me up."

"Come on bro…did you fuck that chick?"

"Nah, bro…I swear on my kids I didn't. I ain't fucking with her like that. But I just sent you the screenshot of what her slow ass sent Kyn."

"Damn bro…Kyn ready to go off on ya ass. Then the bitch had the nerve to tag you in it." Luke chuckled.

"Man…this shit ain't funny."

"Yes, the fuck it is. That's what the fuck you get for fucking with that stupid ass broad. You better get her ass straight before you lose Kyn. Now take ya ass home and fix this shit."

No other words were spoken. I just hung the phone up and made my way to my crib. I hope she didn't go off on my ass. After breaking every traffic violation. I was pulling up in front of my crib. Kyndall's car was still there, so I knew she didn't leave my black ass.

When I walked in the crib, she was sitting on the couch breastfeeding Cassidy. I walked in scared as hell 'cause I didn't know what she was goin' to say.

"Hey, baby…how was your night?" She asked a little too calm for my liking.

"My night was cool. I spent time with Nya and CJ watching movies then I fell asleep on the couch."

She didn't say a word; she burped Cass and got up to put her in her bassinet. Then she turned to me and walked over to where I was standing. She then kissed me on my lips. To say I was shook was an understatement. Her being so calm was scaring the hell out of me.

"Look, I'mma tell you this one time and one time only. You better get her the fuck in check Cash. I've been chilling on the strength of her being CJ's mother, but I ain't gone be taking no disrespect. I'm not gone be goin' through the same shit that I went through with Keem. My heart can't take that shit any more. So, 'cause I trust you enough to know you ain't that stupid to let her ruin what we got goin' on, at least I would hope you weren't that stupid, this was ya pass though. So, if you did do anything, make this your last time. 'Cause next time you gon' come in here and Cass and I will be gone. You already know my track record I'll leave in the blink of an eye, and this time I won't come the fuck back.

Now since you got a good night's rest, take care of her while I take a bath then a nap." Kyndall said in a calm tone and walked away.

I didn't have shit to say to that. I knew one thing. I didn't want her to be taking my baby and leaving me. So, I wasn't doing any more fuck-ups. From now on, when I dropped CJ off I was bringing somebody with me.

I walked over to my baby and kissed the top of her head. Then, I took my shoes off and flopped down on my couch. All I wanted to do was watch my baby sleep and relax.

******

The smell of fried chicken, baked mac, and greens invaded my nostrils. I looked up and Cass was in her swing in front of the TV. I knew Kyn must have been in the kitchen. I jumped up and made my way to the bathroom so I can shower, and maybe dinner will be done. After taking care of my hygiene, I went back downstairs, and Cass was sleep so I laid her in her bassinet. Then made my way into the kitchen.

"Hey beautiful…what you in here cooking?"

"All of your favorites. Are you ready to eat?"

"Yes…I'm starving, and about earlier, I wanted to apologize. I swear on my kids nothing happened and you don't have to never worry about me treating you like Keem did. I have seen first off how that shit hurt you. Remember, I was the shoulder that you cried on most of the time. All my life I've been waiting to get ya ass, and now that I have you, I'mma make sure I do my best to make you happy. I love you, Kyndall, and I plan on loving you until my casket drops." I assured her.

"I love you, too, baby, and I know you didn't do anything with her 'cause ya ass ain't crazy. If I had any kind of thought that you did anything with that hoe, I would have been gone. Like I told you earlier, just get that bitch straight before I fuck her simple ass up."

Kyndall and I sat at the table and enjoyed our dinner. We talked about future shit. I even told her about the family vacation we were going to take real soon. I couldn't wait; we all needed to get away, especially me. Between work and Nadia's stupid ass, I was going to drive myself insane.

Chapter Twelve

Keys

"Baby, have you seen my wallet? I can't find it," I yelled as I walked through the house. I knew that Chrissy was going to start fussing 'cause she was always getting on me for just sitting shit down anywhere. Hell, it's my house. I feel that I should be able to lay my shit where I want and it still be there.

"Here is your wallet, Keys," she said pointing to the kitchen counter. I just dropped my head 'cause I could tell by the look on her face that she was going to get started.

"You need to keep up with your shit. What would you have done if I was already gone? You not gon' learn until you lose it and can't find it." She was moving around the kitchen wearing her workout clothes. I swear to you that shit looked like someone painted it on her. I was happy that she worked out at home. I would hate to have to kill a nigga for trying to get at my girl.

"Come here," I demanded. She made her way to me slowly. Since she was moving so slow, I pulled her. When she was where I wanted her, I grabbed her fat ass. It was so soft.

"Damn baby, you wet as hell," I told her, and I rubbed her clit. I had control over her body, and I loved that shit. I guess I was bullshitting because she damn near pulled me by my dick trying to get it in her.

"Shhhhh," was all that she was able to get out. It was something about her that made a nigga nut fast and I hated that shit. Soon as she started rotating her hips, it was over. I was releasing all in her shit. I knew that sooner or later her ass was going to be pregnant. Just as I was pulling out of her, she kissed me causing my dick to brick back up. As bad as I wanted to slide back in her, I knew that I had to get going. Cash ass hated when people showed up late.

"Baby, I'm finna head out. Call me if you need me. When I get back, we can go and get something to eat," I told her as I headed to the front of the house.

"Ok. I'm going to go and see my mom and go to the bank. I should be back way before you," she told me. I looked back and she was standing in the doorway naked. She knew what she was doing. I just shook my head and walked out of the door. Since I wasn't far from where we were meeting, I decided to roll me a blunt. Once I was done, I headed to my destination. I pulled up to the new warehouse that Cash had just purchased. It was cars everywhere. That meant that everyone was here, which was unusual. Normally, there were two different meetings. One for the legal side and one for the illegal side.

"What's good?" I spoke to everyone as I walked in and made my way to Cash's office. He was still there smiling at his phone. I was in love, but that nigga had me beat.

"Damn nigga. Can you smile any harder? "I joked. He looked up at me then busted out laughing.

"Kyn ass just sent me a picture of Cass. That little girl is my twin," he beamed. I couldn't wait to have that feeling.

"So, what's this meeting about. You never have both sides together."

"I know. I just needed to set some new rules and didn't want to have to say the shit twice," he admitted. "Also, I wanted you to see all the people that work for me. Since you are taking on more responsibility, I need them to know who you are. You know how motherfuckers will try and get over if they can."

"Real shit," I replied as he got up to head out of his office. When he walked into the room, all the talking stopped instantly. Just as he was getting ready to start talking, Luke walked in. He took a seat by the door and Cash got started with the meeting.

Luke

Today was not my day; Shawnee ass had an attitude and Joi was sick. That mixed together was a disaster. I had no idea what was up with Shawnee. I guess it was just the baby. When she woke up she was a little moody but by the time I was leaving the house she was spazzing out. I was ready for her to have the baby so that she could get back to herself. Then Joi has a fever. I took her to the park yesterday and Shawnee swore that was why she was sick. She didn't want Joi going to the park often because she said that kids held germs.

Me: *What you want me to bring back to eat?*

Wifey: *I want Mcdonalds fries, some nuggets for Wendys, and some Waffle House*

I didn't reply back because I knew that what I wanted to say was going to make her mad all over again. The only thing that helped her get over her attitude was when food was involved. She always wanted some crazy ass shit. It was never simple. The shit was rubbing off on Joi.

I sat at the door listening to Cash speak. I was happy that he was back to his old self. That nigga damn near going crazy. As he talked, I took time to watch all of the people in the room. I found that people's facial expressions told how they really felt. We had every person that was on our payroll here.

For some reason, my attention kept falling on one of the new niggas that had just started working for us. His attention was on his phone and not Cash. That shit pissed me off more than I already was. That simply told me that what Cash was saying didn't mean shit to him.

"Yo Cash. I think that you need to stop talking and let this nigga finish what he doing," Keys yelled out pulling me for my thoughts. I looked up to see him standing near the nigga that I was just talking about.

"Nah, I'm good," was all the nigga said.

"Let's see what's more important than getting some money," I said, taking his phone out his hand. I scanned what he was saying and started seeing red. I took the phone to Cash so that he could see for himself. I initially thought to read it out loud, but I didn't. There was a lot of people here that worked in the Pharmacy, so I didn't want them to see that side of Cash. What they didn't know was that they were working for a real savage ass nigga.

Cash read it and kept going on with the meeting as if it was nothing. Once he was done talking, he dismissed everyone that works in the pharmacy. He made sure that they were all gone then he took a seat at the head of the table. I knew at that moment that he was about to click the fuck out. The nigga was sitting there looking as if he wasn't bothered. See, most of these niggas didn't see Cash often. He was behind the scenes most of the time. Cash took care of the legal side of things.

Everyone in the room was on edge. It was quiet as hell. You would probably be able to hear a pin drop. Cash was just sitting there looking at his phone.

"Keys show me what you would do in this situation," Cash said as he pecked on his phone.

"Well, we all know what happens to snakes and rats," Keys added. Before he could say another word, Cash blew a hole in the nigga's head. The whole time that he was standing there he was smirking. When I took his phone, he was texting Nadia. But what he didn't know was that I had also looked at the text right under that one. He was an informant. Had he not been a dumb ass nigga he would have gotten us knocked but because he wanted to be cocky, he had fucked that up.

Once everyone was gone and everything was cleaned up, I headed to get my baby her food. I had been gone for almost three hours so I knew that she would be calling soon. It didn't take me long to get everything that she wanted. Once I had it, I stopped to get Joi some popsicles. When I pulled up to my house my mom's car was in the driveway. She had been coming over a lot since Shawnee was getting bigger. "Baby," I called out. Before I could get all the way in the house Joi flew to me. Her ass was acting a lot better than she was doing before I left.

"Daddy, Mommy made me feel better," she told me as I picked her up. I made my way to the kitchen, and she was sitting at the island working on her laptop.

"Hey baby," I greeted her. She took the food from my hand without saying a word. I just stood there as she spread all of the food out on the island. It took her no time to dive in. While she was eating, I went to find my mother.

She was in the movie room on the phone with one of her friends running her mouth as always. "Hey, Ma."

"Hey, son. Why are you holding Joi? She can walk," my mom fussed. She was always fussing about me holding my baby. I ignored her like I always did. Joi was my child and if I wanted to baby her then that's what I was going to do.

I sat down and Joi grabbed the remote. She put *Frozen* on as always and got comfortable in the seat that was next to me. I guess that made my mom mad because she got up and left.

As always, I started watching the movie with my baby. I didn't realize I had drifted off till I felt Shawnee's lips touch mines.

"How was your meeting baby?" she asked sitting on my lap. See, this was the shit that pissed me off; her ass was just mad, but now that she got some food, she just fine.

"It was ok; some nigga wanted to play but that's over and done. How are you and my son?"

"We good; was just missing you. I want to go and see Kyndall and the baby. Can you take me?" she asked. She knew damn well that I wasn't going to tell her no.

"Yes, baby. Are you taking Joi or leaving her here with Mama?"

"She can stay here if she wants. I just wanted to get out of the house for a while." I just nodded and headed to see if my mama wanted Joi to stay with her.

"Ma?"

"What?" she answered like I was getting on her nerves.

"We about to go to Cash house. Do you want me to take Joi with me?" I asked.

"Why would you take her out there in the cold when she already sick?" My mom fussed. I didn't worry with replying. I just walked off. When I made it to our room, Shawnee was fully dressed in some tights and one of my Gucci t-shirts. On her feet, she had on some Gucci bowling shoes. She looked good as always.

"That's why I can never find my shirts," I said walking in the room and sitting on the bed.

"Well, I can't fit none of my clothes and there is no way that I'm going to buy new stuff when I won't be this size forever," she said before kissing me. She knew that was going to get my dick hard. I just sat there because I needed to get my life in order before going downstairs.

Chapter Thirteen

Kyndall

I was glad Shawnee was coming over. I needed to talk to her about something before I brought it to Cash. Shit has been crazy since I had Cass and we decided to move together and make shit official. The crazy part was I was getting sick and tired of Nadia's trifling ass and I feel like we had CJ so much he might as well live here with us. I wasn't sure what Cash was going to say about that, though, since they both were so small. CJ was six months and Cass being a month the shit would be mad hard, but I felt like we would be able to handle it. We had a great support system, so I didn't see it being that bad. Cash would just have to be home more.

I smiled at the thought of how my life had changed so drastically in so little time. The only thing that worried me at this point was I had a feeling Keem was going to pop up. No one has heard from him in a while. It was like he just dropped off of the face of the earth. I hoped to God he stayed where the hell he was 'cause we didn't need these problems.

"Hey suga...where you at?" Shawnee yelled, walking her big ass in my house like she paid bills here.

"I'm in the living room fatty, and what are you doing letting ya self in my damn house?"

"You gave me a key, hoe, so why not?"

"I gave you the damn key for an emergency. Keep it up and I'mma take it back."

"Bitch...it was an emergency. I'm fat and pregnant and I can't stay on my feet too long."

"Yeah...whatever. Where's my princess at?"

"I left her home with mama. She's not feeling good and I didn't want her to pass it on to my Cassy Pooh. Where she at anyway?"

"Her spoiled butt is in her crib sleeping."

I looked at Shawnee and smiled at how beautiful she was. Her belly was so round and big. She wore her pregnancy so well.

"So, what's going on; what did you wanna talk to me about?"

"A couple of different things. For starters, do you think they killed Keem? It's funny how we haven't heard anything from him in a minute."

"Shit, I don't know; they may have. But you know they never going to tell us if they did. What made you think of him."

"I was going through some paperwork and checking all my accounts and the joint one was empty," I said while shaking my head.

"That nigga ain't shit for that. If they did kill him, I hope they find his body soon. So, you can get your insurance policy money." Shawnee giggled.

I couldn't do anything but laugh at her simple ass. I always think about how things went, and I wish it could have gone in a different direction. Who would have ever thought my ex-husband would have been such an asshole? Then, when Cash told me how he did ol' girl I thought of him as a monster; the shit was sad. To even think I loved a man like him was crazy.

"Yeah, all this shit is really crazy; who would have ever thought he would be anything like how he turned out."

"Yeah, he was crazy. That's why I never liked his sorry ass. I only dealt with him 'cause of you. But enough about him. What's on ya mind? I know you didn't call me over here to talk about that fuck boy." I laughed at Shawnee's mean ass.

"I was thinking about all the shit we've been going through with Nadia, and I'm going to talk to Cash about us getting custody of CJ."

"I mean it's going to be hard 'cause they both so young, but y'all got him most of the time anyway. That bitch was a fucking egg donor. Between you and Cash mama, y'all gone be the ones CJ calls mommy. Instead of going through the halftime shit with her, take him. I don't see anything wrong with that, and I know Cash will be all for it."

"You really think so? I thought he might not wanna do it 'cause of them both being so young."

"Girl please, Cash will do anything to have all of y'all under one roof. Nadia is getting on his damn nerves, and he not trying to risk ya, stubborn ass running off when shit gets too much with Nadia. This time if you run off you gon' be taking his precious Cass and he might kill ya ass." Shawnee assured me.

"Girl bye, Cash ain't doing shit."

"Girl, last time you left he was fucking tripping. He drove me and Luke crazy. He didn't even wanna wash his ass. All he wanted to do is spend his nights in the streets and kill people. So, yeah if you ever take his daughter, he gon' drag ya ass right back here. One thing you don't mess with is Cash money, his kids, and his Kyndall."

I looked at Shawnee like she was crazy, but I knew deep down inside she was telling the truth. I was gon' talk to Cash as soon as he got home.

"Ok... I'm talking to him about it. What's up with Meia and the rehab?"

"She's doing really good, but I told Luke I wasn't going back up there. So, he and mama had been taking Joi up there. From my understanding, they helping her with housing and a job. I wish her the best, but I don't think I ever want Joi to live with her again. I don't think my heart would ever be able to take it. Even if she gets clean. I know I may sound selfish, but she put her in a bad situation. I could never look at her any different than a fuck up, and if I wasn't pregnant when that shit went down, I would have probably fucked her up."

"You have gotten so attached to that little girl. I don't think I will ever let her have her back. Shit, she lucky her ass ain't in jail or stinking in an ocean somewhere. So, I don't think you'll ever have to worry about her crazy ass. I just hope she gets her life together for Joi."

"Well, the last time I saw her she seemed sincere, so I hope she takes this as a learning experience and gets her life straight. Ouch…" Shawnee yelled causing me to jump up.

"What's the matter boo? Are you ok?"

"Girl, I swear I got a ten-pound football player in my belly. He be kicking the shit out of me." I giggled while shaking my head.

As soon as I went to sit back down, Cass started to cry. I told Shawnee I would be right back and headed to the nursery to get her. The conversation with Shawnee made me feel so much better. Tonight, over a nice dinner I was going to bring it to Cash to see how he felt about it.

Nadia

"Damn bitch you need to clean up. Every time I come over here it looks worse. How do you have yo, baby in this shit?" Karen asked when she walked in the door. She annoyed me; she was the reason that I was like this and she wanted to judge me. Hell, she had more damn kids than me and her house was never clean. I looked around my living room and it was a mess. Just as I was getting ready to reply CJ started crying like always. That was why his ass needed to be with his daddy. Cash was always just dropping him off and picking him up at his own discretion. I hated that shit. That meant that I couldn't get high.

"Ughhh," was all I said before getting up and going to check on CJ. When I walked in the room, he was standing in his bed crying. "Lil boy what is ya, problem today," I asked as I got him out of bed.

"Well, hell at least his room clean," she said, taking a seat in the rocking chair. I just rolled my eyes because she always had some shit to say.

"So, you get out tonight?" she asked. I knew that's why her walking ass came over here. She wanted to go out, but she didn't have a car. I wanted to tell her ass no, but I thought about the fact that I could get high for free since I was the one driving. The only thing was I didn't know if Cash was going to come and get CJ today.

"I will let you know. I have to see if he is coming to get CJ." It took me no time to get him back to sleep. Once he was back in his bed, I headed to the front so that I could clean up. She just took a seat and talked my ears off about a whole lot of nothing. She knew every damn body business but her own.

"So, I meet this nigga the other day. He wants us to come and kick it with him before we go out. That way we can get high on his dime," she said catching my attention. I had tuned her ass out. Just as I was going to reply, my sister called. I just looked at the phone and kept sweeping the floor. I didn't have time for them today. Just thinking about it I needed to call Cash. Otherwise, CJ was going to be here by himself for a few hours. He would be ok; he would sleep anyway.

After I was done cleaning, I took a seat on the couch so that I could call Cash. When I called, he didn't answer so I got on Instagram so that I could see what his other baby mama was up to. All her ass did was post since she had her baby. I started seeing red when I saw a picture that she posted of her daughter and my baby. They were both dressed alike in Gucci. You could tell that the picture was a professional one. She was really pushing it. I should have beat her ass back when she was always around. I think that's what hurt the most. I knew they liked each other but he kept saying that I was overthinking. One thing that I used to tell him was that a woman's intuition was never wrong. I was the one that he was supposed to be with.

I closed out of the app and called his ass again. I was going to keep calling until he answered. It was like I was getting madder and madder every time his voicemail picked up.

"Damn bitch you ok?" my homegirl asked. I wanted to tell her what I was going off on, but I was embarrassed. She is living the life that I was supposed to be living. That wasn't fair. She should have just stayed with her husband. She was the reason that I was using drugs. I was going to make her and Cash pay.

"Yes, I will be good." We sat there and talked and got high. I knew that I had no business getting high while my baby was here, but I needed it after seeing all those pictures of them acting like one big happy ass family.

I looked at the time and seen that it was almost midnight. That was my queue to roll. I didn't worry about going to check on CJ because I knew that he was sleep.

"Let's go, bitch," I said waking Karen up. She was so high that she had fallen asleep standing at the door. She looked herself over in the mirror and then walked out the door. I guess she needed that little nap because when we got in the car, she was wide awake and getting on my last damn nerve. Her ass was talking a mile a minute. It took us damn near forty-five minutes to make it to the address that she had in the GPS. So, my attitude was on ten. I hated driving and she knew that.

The hotel that we pulled up to looked run down. Hell, I didn't really want to go in but the idea of getting high overclouded my judgment. After she got out the car so did I. We made our way to the room. When the door opened I could have run.

"If it isn't Nadia. I would ask how life is treating you, but I can see," Keem said. There was no way that this nigga was still alive. Hell, I thought that he was good and dead, especially since no one has seen his ass in months. I bet he didn't know that his wife had just had a baby with his best friend. It's cool because he was getting ready to find out.

Chapter Fourteen

Cash

"Baby, can you get Cass while I get in the shower?"
Kyndall asked as she walked in my office holding my baby
girl. She was getting so big and I was loving every moment
of it. She was the prettiest little girl.

"Come on, baby girl, so mommy can get in the shower. We
don't want her around here smelling like I garbage can."
Kyndall slapped my arm as she made her way out of my
office.

Since I was in here so much, I had Cass' bouncer in here as
well as a playpen for CJ. I had been working all damn day.
I had to cut my phone on vibrate just so that I could get
some shit done. Otherwise, I wouldn't have gotten anything
done. There had been so much going that I had to play
catch up. I was finally good, so I pulled my phone out the
drawer. I saw that I had twenty-seven missed calls from
Nadia. There was a few from Luke but I'm sure if
something was wrong, he would have called Kyndall.

I called Nadia back but didn't get an answer so I decided
that I would take Cass to her room and bathe her. I was so
proud to be a father. By the time that she was done in the
shower, Cassidy was in the bed. She was such a good baby.

"That's a lot of ass," I said as I watched Kyndall bend
overlooking for something in the drawer. Just I said that I
thought about the fact that her six weeks was up. Seeing
that my dick was brick hard I dropped my gym short and
slid right in. She didn't know what had hit her ass.

"Cash," she moaned out. I swear my baby was the fucking
best. I don't see what the fuck Keem was thinking.

"Damn baby," was all I was able to say. She was throwing
that ass back driving my ass crazy. She had some good shit.
By the time I was done with her, she was ready to take a
nap. We showered again then I went to check on CJ. Nadia
had called too many times for her not to be answering. As I

made my way to the car, I called Luke to see what he was doing.

"Aye nigga what the hell you doing?" I asked him soon as he answered.

"Shit just headed to the house. What you got up."

"Finna go and check on CJ. Nadia called a nigga a million times and now she not answering, you know I don't trust that bitch so I'm going to check on my youngin'."

"Aw shit. I will meet you there cause you know how yo ass is," he laughed. That nigga knew me too well. She did as well so I don't know why she wanna play with me.

"Nigga, I got this," I tried assuring him. That nigga just laughed and hung up on me. I didn't worry about calling back. I just headed to Nadia's house. When I pulled up there were three police cars in front of the house. Just as I got out the car, Luke was pulling up. We both rushed to the house.

"Sir, you can't go in there," The officer said as we both walked in the house. My son was in there, so I wasn't paying hi no fucking mind. I was going in that house. We both kept walking. When we walked in there was an officer holding CJ. Soon as he seen me, he started crying.

"You must be dad?" she flirted. I didn't reply. I just reached for my baby. "We got a call from the neighbor. She said that she saw the mother leave hours ago. She said she didn't think anything of it until she heard the baby crying," she told me. I hated when Nadia picked this house because the neighbor's was so close. Hell, now I was grateful for that.

"You have to wait for DFYS to come before we can let you leave with him. They may have to keep him as well. He was left unattended. When we got here, he had rolled out of the bed and was on the floor."

I was hot and Luke must have sensed it because he took over the conversation. "Ok, so he wasn't in his bed?" Luke asked.

"No sir, he was in the master bedroom on the floor. The door was unlocked as well," she advised. My blood was boiling. Nadia had really fucked up. I was doing my best to give her the benefit of the doubt. I pulled out my phone to call her but didn't get an answer. That shit pissed me off worse. Anything could have happened.

We sat around for an hour waiting on DFYS and Nadia still hadn't shown up. I had been calling her phone nonstop. I didn't want to call Kyndall, because I knew that she was going to be pissed. She didn't like for me to send him here, but she felt that he deserved to spend some time with his mother. I already felt that something was up with her. She had been acting weird. Hell, I was shocked that her house was even this clean. That was something that I have had to tell her about every time I came by. She was really falling off and that was a no-go for me.

"Hey baby," she answered.

"I just came over to check on CJ because Nadia had been calling all day, but I was working. When I got here the police was here and he was alone," I explained. She was quiet so I knew that she was thinking.

"Ok baby, I'm on the way. Ma just got here so she can keep CJ," was all that she said. I knew that she was going to come running for CJ. She loved him just as much as she loved Cass.

Luke just sat at the door on the phone. I'm sure that he was talking to Shawnee. The way that his face was looking I knew that she was on the phone talking shit. That's all she did. I was so happy when I saw the Social Worker walk in because I was ready to go home. Just as the social worker walked in so did Kyndall. She was looking like she was ready for war. Soon as CJ laid eyes Kyndall he reached out for her.

The social worker thought that she was Nadia. After we explained to her who Kyn was, she proceeded to ask a million questions. I prayed that they found Nadia before I did because I was going to kill her ass. Luke called me outside, so I left Kyndall and the case worker to talk. When we walked out the door, he handed me the phone.

"Hello," I spoke in the receiver.

"Nigga you will never guess who I just saw," Keys said.

"Who?"

"Ya boy Keem and the nigga was with yo hoe ass baby mama," he added. That had my full attention. What the fuck were they doing together?

"Do you still know their location, or you saw them in passing?

"I'm right behind them. You know I've been looking for this fuck nigga, and I refused to let him out of my sight. So, when they stop. I'll hit y'all to let you know my location. I'm killing this nigga on sight so don't take too long." Keys said.

"We got you, we on our way right now," I assured Keys.

Keem

"I told you bitches that I was in the hideout. I can't be doing all this traveling around." I snapped at Nadia and her stupid ass friend.

When I got with the dude that was giving me all the information on Cash, I learned that Nadia and he had a son. He and my wife had a fucking daughter together. The shit fucked me up emotionally, being as though my little princess died. I found out who Nadia ran with and when I realized she was on some other shit; I got her friend to lure her my way. All I wanted to do was fuck, get high, and use her to get at Cash. These two sorry ass mutha fuckas, living they best life and I'm out here hiding out.

"Just chill out daddy...we going to my spot. Her baby daddy doesn't even know me."

"Who says my baby daddy is looking for him?" Nadia asked while giving us both the side-eye. What she didn't know was me and her friend had hooked up a couple times and I put her on to everything. The shady bitch got her here in no time. All I had to do was get her high and fuck the shit out of her. She told me the shit that her and Nadia was into, and I just shook my head. Her dumb ass waited til after she had the baby to get worse. Nadia ass always been on that good bullshit but popping pills and sniffing coke wasn't her thing.

"I was sitting back listening to you talk. I just put two and two together." She lied.

"Why we end up coming to your house? I thought we were heading out. I left my son in the house for this bullshit." Nadia sassed.

"Wait, you did what? You stupid bitch. What is wrong with you?"

"Cash wanna always be up under your dumb ass wife and that little ugly baby. That he forgets all about me and CJ." Nadia sucked her teeth.

"I know I'm about to get the fuck away from y'all now. If Cash found out that little baby is home alone, he is going to kill ya dumb ass."

"Cash doesn't know shit yet. He too far up ya wife's ass. Now stop being a bitch ass nigga and let's just go have a good time." I didn't give a damn what Nadia was talking about; as soon as we got to our destination I was dipping off. The Cash I know probably got somebody following us right now as we speak. In less than five minutes paranoia had come over me, and I started looking in the rearview. I then noticed there was a car following us. Nadia must have noticed me looking out of the windows.

"What's wrong with you? Why you keep looking out the windows like that?"

"Think this black car is following us. The windows are tinted, so we can't even see who it is. Make a sharp right up here. If the car does the same, then we know we're definitely being followed." Just like I knew, as soon as we made that sharp right the car did the same.

"Shit...the car is following us." Nadia snapped.

"Well, you better speed the fuck up and try to leave his ass."

"Don't worry. I got this." Nadia assured us and sped off.

"Try to get to a busy area or near a police station. When the driver notices that, he will for sure turn around if it's one of Cash's goons. They hate the police station." Nadia did as she was told and hopped on the next highway that led to downtown. Down there was always swarming with cops being as though the hospital, police station, and county jail was right down there. I knew we would be fine.

Ten minutes went by and we were pulling into the police station. The black car didn't follow us into the parking lot, but we had to chill for a minute to make sure his ass wasn't parked around the corner somewhere. Nadia was sitting there looking at me all crazy. When her phone rang, I looked at her and by the look that was now was on her face, I knew it had to be Cash calling her stupid ass.

"Well, it looks like ya dumb ass about to be hiding too. 'Cause when Cash gets ya ass you're as good as dead." I said while shaking my head.

"Y'all got too damn much going on. All I'm trying to do is get high and fuck. I ain't trying to be out here running from people and shit. Nadia, every time a nigga find out who your baby daddy is they be ready to bounce. Shit, who the fuck is this nigga. He blowing my shit, now when are we leaving? I hate the police station." Nadia's friend complained.

"Girl shut the fuck up. You the reason I'm in this shit now. Fucking around with you and all these damn drugs. Not everybody got family that'll keep they kids, so they can run around and get high all the damn time."

"Fuck you bitch…now drop me off at home. I'll find me some new dick and pussy." The friend fussed.

Shit, a nigga was kind of pissed. I was about to have a good as time with these two freaks. But since, baby girl wanted to go home. I hoped Nadia dropped her whining ass home. That way, me and her could find somewhere to go and catch up.

"You don't have to tell me twice. I'm dropping ya hoe ass right off and don't fucking call me tomorrow bitch."

"Don't worry I won't."

Nadia looked at me and I gave her the ok to go. It had been about twenty minutes, and I knew dude wasn't still following us. We hurried and dropped homegirl off then we peeled off.

"Where will we go now?" Nadia asked.

"You know I'm on the run, so I haven't even been in the city. I been down in Atlantic City. If you want, you can come with me and let a couple of days go by then we can head back and figure this thing out together. Are you down with that?" I asked.

"I know when Cash gets to me, he's going to kill me. I'm going to miss my son, but I know he's not going to give him back to me after this stunt anyway. Only way I could see him doing that is if I'm ready to get some help when I get back. I know that's not going to happen. I'm so depressed that the drugs take my mind off of everything. Why did she have to take my man? Not only did she do that, she turned around and had a baby by him. My feelings are so hurt. I have been nothing but a fuck up all my life." Nadia said with a tear stained face.

"Stop crying girl; everything is going to be ok. Let's go. I have a friend that we could stay with; she lives in Absecon, New Jersey. Not far from Atlantic City. She's good people; she's been looking out for me while I've been hiding out."

"Ok cool…put the address in my GPS and let's go."

I did what Nadia said and we headed out. I shot, baby girl a text to let her know I was bringing a friend with me. Once I told her it was a female, she was all for it. I wasn't saying I was bringing her in for sexual reasons, but since she got excited, I knew she would have food, drinks and plenty of coke waiting on us by the time we got there. I would wait til tomorrow to discuss our plan to get at Cash and Kyndall for ruining our life.

Chapter Fifteen

Keys

Saying I was pissed off would be an understatement right now. I was so fucking mad that I let those assholes get one up on me. How the fuck did I let this shit happen? I knew I was dirty, so being downtown wasn't the place for me. If I didn't have guns in my car I would have stayed and waited for them to come out of the police station parking lot. I knew that shit wasn't nobody, but Keem's bitch ass that told them to do that shit. Hell, Nadia didn't even know I was following her.

I called Luke and told him the news. He told me not to worry about it, and to go home and chill with my girl. Tomorrow, we gon' meet up to see if we could get somebody on the hunt. He assured me that he would put a cost on that nigga's head.

"Hey baby! How you feeling today?" Chrissy asked when I walked in my house.

"I'm good baby…what you still doing up?" I asked while pulling her in for a hug.

"I couldn't sleep, so I just came down here to wait for you. Are you hungry? I cooked dinner for you earlier."

"Yeah, I could eat. Let me go get out of these clothes and I'll be right back."

"Alright, I'll have your food heated for you when you get back down here."

I made my way up to my room and stripped out of my clothes. I threw on a pair of ballers and a wife beater. I looked around the room and noticed that Chrissy had done, cleaned up and changed the sheet on the bed again. I never lived with a female until now. At first, it took some getting used to, but now it be, what I need after a long day in these streets. After what I went through today, I'm mad as fuck, but when I walked in the door and saw her pretty face, it made me push all the street shit in the back of my head.

Hearing Chrissy call my name brought me out of my thoughts and I headed down to the dining room to eat my food.

"Here you go baby. I made some chicken alfredo, garlic bread, and fresh spinach on the side. Would you like a beer or iced tea?"

"Thank you, ma! The iced tea will be fine." Once she handed me my plate, she grabbed herself a cup of tea and sat right across from me.

"How was your day?" I asked her, sparking up conversation.

"Boring as usual... I think I wanna get back on the work scene. What do you think about that?"

"What type of work are you looking to do?"

"I mean I never really looked into anything since daddy always took care of me. Then I messed that up dealing with Keem's ass. So, now I'm just trying to figure out what I wanna do. I mean I'm good at selling shit. So, maybe I'll do something like that."

"Well, I was thinking about buying a bunch of houses and flipping them. I be seeing so many abandoned houses in the city. If I can get them fixed up there would be less place for bullshit to happen. We can rent them or sell them. What you think about that? You could be home doing the class online for real estate."

I didn't wanna force my dream on her, but I knew she had no clue. So, I just put it in the air. She didn't have to do it if she didn't want to. I thought it would be a great opportunity for the both of us. I didn't plan on leaving the street shit alone. I did wanna clean my money up some. So, that if something happened to me, she would be able to live comfortably.

"I like that idea; that way we could both be in business together."

"Yup my point exactly. Whenever you ready to get it started let me know."

"I'm ready to start as soon as possible. I'll check around for the classes I need to take tomorrow. I'll also do a business class as well. Is it ok if I turn the extra room into an office?"

"You can do whatever you want ma. This isn't just my house; it's ours."

After we sat and talked a little while longer, I was finished eating, and she was yawning like she was tired. I got up and cleaned my plate off then we headed upstairs.

"Do you wanna shower with me?" Chrissy asked, getting on her tippy toes and wrapping her arms around my neck. I stared into her eyes right before kissing her lips.

"Yeah, come on, let's go."

Once we made it to the bathroom, I undressed Chrissy and then myself. We shared a long passionate kiss, while we waited for the water to get the right temperature. When I figured we were satisfied we both hopped in. As soon as we got in, we gave each other an intense stare. I then grabbed her by her neck and pushed her up against the wall. I applied a little pressure just enough to get that pussy extra wet just the way I liked it. I grabbed her leg with my free hand and lifted it to give myself easy access to slide right in my pussy. When Chrissy figured out what I was doing, she rested her foot on the tub, while I began to give her long, hard, deep strokes.

"Mmm...baby just like that." Chrissy cooed while I gave her the business.

When I sped up the pace, I felt her juices running out of her. Yeah, I had her body doing all types of shit. I just kept drilling in and out of her until I felt her body jerking once again.

"Turn that ass around ma. I wanna hit it from the back." I barked.

Chrissy did as she was told, and I slid right back into her opening. She still kept her leg on the ledge while I continued to buss her ass. I then moved my hand to her clit and began to play with it while I fucked her from behind.

"Fuck Keys… fuck me harder baby…fuck me harder."

"That's it ma…tell me how to fuck you. Are you ready to cum again?"

"Yesss…baby I'm ready to cum again." Chrissy moaned out in ecstasy. I felt her pussy muscles contracting on my dick, and I knew this session was coming to an end. So, I started moving in and out of her in a fast motion. Making sure to hit her spot. I was going hard and I couldn't hold back anymore just as that thought came to mind, I felt her body start to shake.

"Come ma; let's buss this nut together." The minute those words left my mouth, we both came long and hard. I had to hold Chrissy up so she wouldn't fall. Once I made sure she was good and both her feet were on the floor, I grabbed her face and brought her face to mine. Then, I kissed her lips.

"I love you ma!"

"I love you more Keys." After that, we washed each other then made our way to bed.

Kyndall

It had been a couple of days since the shit went down with CJ. The authorities had let us bring him home with us. Since there was no sign of his mom and she was now declared unfit, Cash and I had talked about getting custody of him. We had agreed on giving her a chance at first before we decided to do it. Now I was all for it; she had her chance and she fucked up. I would just have to be a stay-at-home mother which is fine with me. Shawnie and I were thinking about going into business together running online boutiques, which is cool since she makes the clothes. I would be the distributor.

"What, you doing in here?" Cash asked while walking into the bedroom.

"Just relaxing; both the babies are sleeping finally. They both drove me crazy today."

"I told you I would hire a nanny, but you keep telling me no. I know you're a great mother, and I appreciate all you do for CJ, but baby you need help around here. So, let me get you some."

Cash was right. I didn't want any nanny in my damn home, but I did need help. Having two babies' months apart was hard work. I barely had time for myself. Hell, I barely had time for my man. I miss that dick so much. I knew that if we did get one, she was going to be old. I didn't want no woman in my shit with my man. Chrissy fucked that up. The only woman that I trusted around my man was Shawnee. I knew for a fact that she would never do anything like that. Hell, he better be glad that I didn't go and fire every female that worked for him.

"Alright, we could start looking for one since this looks like it's going to be long-term."

"Yeah, I haven't heard anything from her ass. The neighbors said she hasn't been home either."

"I'm glad we don't have no fucking nosey ass neighbors like that," I told him as I combed my hair into a ponytail. I hadn't been to the salon since I had my baby, and I was more than ready to go. I didn't want Cash to be looking at other women the way that Keem did. I wanted to make sure that I stayed on point.

"Shit, me too. If we did, they would think that I was beating you rather than beating that fat ass pussy," he joked. I just laughed because he was always talking nasty.

"You so damn nasty," I said kissing him. He grabbed my ass causing my center to get wet. I looked at him and he was smirking. I knew that meant that he was doing that shit on purpose. Before I knew it we were going at it as always.

******

"Bitch, you look like you about to fucking bust," I said as I walked into Luke and Shawnee's house. Her ass was so damn big. I felt bad for my friend because she looked so uncomfortable.

"Shut up bitch. Don't act like you wasn't just looking the same damn way. Give me my baby," she said, taking Cass from my arms.

We were at her house because they were getting ready to throw some food on the grill. I seemed to be still hungry all the damn time. I prayed that it stopped because I didn't want to be as big as a damn house. Cash swore that he liked the weight, but I hated it. I was almost one-eighty and that was for the birds. I wanted to be back to the size that I was before Cassidy's ass.

While she was holding Cassidy, I took that time to make the baked beans. When I walked in the kitchen, I seen that she hadn't cooked anything. I made my way to the living room. "So, you haven't done shit all day?" I asked.

She just shrugged her shoulder. If it had been just us, I wouldn't have cared but the fact that she had invited plenty of people changed all of that. I just shook my head and went back to the kitchen. I cut on my Pandora and started cooking. I was happy that she had all of the shit that I needed. I looked in the backyard and seen that Luke was already on the grill.

"Baby does CJ have a change of clothes. I want to take him outside, but I know that he will smell like smoke." I sat down the spoon that I was using and went to get the baby bag. I put both of their stuff in one bag. There was no way that I was gon' be walking around with two bags.

"Here, put this one on him. That way when the guest starts coming, he can put his clothes back on," I said handing him a onesie. "And make sure that you leave his socks on," I added.

He grabbed the onesies and walked off. I knew that he was pissed because he hated for me to tell him what to do when it came to the kids. I didn't care though. They were my babies, and I wasn't about to let them get sick. His ass was going to be out in the streets, and I was going to be home with them.

"What's good sis," Luke spoke when he came in the house. I just nodded because I had food in my mouth. He came overlooking in my pot as always. I hated when he and Cash did that. That shit made me feel like they felt that I didn't know what I was doing. "Stop looking like that," Cash fussed as he walked in the kitchen. He was always the one to point out my facial expressions. I just smiled. That was one of the things that I loved; he was always too attentive. He knew all that there was to know about me.

It took me no time to make the beans, spaghetti, potato salad, and mac & chess. I finished just as guests started to arrive. I headed to see what Shawnee and the kids were doing. Joi wasn't feeling good earlier, so she said that she was going to lay her down. I made my way up the stairs and headed straight to her room. When I looked in there, she wasn't there so I knew that she had to have been in Joi's room. When I opened Joi's door, I couldn't do anything but pull my phone out. It was the cutest thing. Shawnee was laying in the middle of Joi's king-sized bed. She had Cassidy in one arm and CJ in the other. Joi was laying on her belly like she was a pillow.

I wanted to wake her, but she looked like she was sleeping good. I just closed the door back and headed down the stairs. The first person that I saw was Chrissy. She was walking in the door with a bottle of wine. I walked straight past her ass like I didn't see her. I still wasn't fucking with her ass. I made a mental note to keep my eye on my man because we all knew how that hoe got down. I would hate to have to kill her ass.

Chapter Sixteen

Nadia

"Ow, just like that Keem," I moaned as Keem hit me from the back. This nigga dick game was the best. That is next to Cash. Just the thought of Cash had my pussy dripping. I missed Cash's ass. I wish that bitch Kyndall would have just stayed where the fuck she was at. It was her fault that I was strung out the way that I was. If she would have stayed gone. I would still be happy and have my man. Then to know that she wanted him so bad that she trapped him with a baby really made me mad.

"Damn, this pussy so wet," he moaned. He was hitting my spot and swear that shit was driving me crazy. The rate he was going, I was going to be in love. He was fucking me good and getting me high, and that was all a girl wanted.

"Shit, a nigga gone nut all in the pussy," he moaned out. Soon as he said that I came all over his dick. Once we were done, I went to get cleaned up. When I walked in the hallway, the girl house that we were at was just standing there.

"I know you from somewhere," she blurted. I just shrugged and walked off. I didn't know her ass and knew damn well that she didn't know me.

Just as I was walking back in the room my phone rang and it was Cash. I knew that he probably had been by my house by now, so I just hit ignore. That was his baby like it was mine, so I didn't need to always have him.

"You wanna hit this," Keem said, handing me the blunt that he was smoking. This nigga was on all kinds of shit. I guess all he wanted was to be high. On the way here he popped a perc, we took two lines and now high ass was smoking weed.

"So, you still be fucking with Cash?" he asked. I just rolled my eyes because Cash was the last thing that I wanted to talk about.

"Naw, not at all." When I looked over, he had a smirk on his face. I wanted to ask what it was about, but I was enjoying my high and I didn't need shit knocking it down. The was laid back on the bed looking good. Keem may not have been a thug ass nigga like Cash and Luke but he was fine. That Kyndall bitch knew how to pick them, that's for sure.

"I don't fuck with that nigga either," he added. I just nodded because there was nothing that I could say back to that. Hell, I didn't care if he dealt with the nigga or not. That was not my business.

"We need to think of a way to get some money. Getting high is not free. I was thinking we can tell the nigga to come and get y'all kid and then have some nigga to follow his ass home and rob him. I know that he won't carry much on him, but he has to have something wherever Kyndall is. Once we rob him, I'm going to kill him and that bitch," Keem finished. I was about to tell him how crazy he was until he pulled out a little bag. That was all that I needed to see. I was down with whatever at that point.

I took one hit and that was it for me. I dropped to my knees so that I could pay him for treating me so good. Anytime that I was high all I wanted to do was fuck. It never failed; my pussy was always tender after because we would fuck for hours.

"Suck that dick baby," he moaned out. I was sucking his shit like my life depended on it. "Bend that pussy over," he demanded. I did as I was told. I knew that he was going to fuck the lining out of me. When it took him a little longer than normal, I turned around to see that nigga getting on his knees. He licked me from my asshole to my pussy. That shit had my mind fucked up. He had never eaten my pussy.

I guess all the shit that he was on had his ass on another level; I wasn't complaining though.

"Damn baby," I managed to get out. He had my words stuck. Like who would have known that this nigga gave head this damn good. I was riding this nigga's face before he knew it. I loved getting my pussy ate.

"This pussy taste so damn good," he mumbled. Before I knew it, I was squirting all over his face. He just smiled and pulled me down onto his dick. I swear I was in love. I would damn near do whatever he asked me to at this point.

Cash

"Nigga, why the hell you over here looking like that?"
Keys asked me as he walked in the backyard.
I had been calling Nadia's hoe ass all day. It has been
almost two weeks since she left my son at home alone and
a week since the day that Keys seen her. I had niggas on the
street looking for her and Keem ass. They both had to see
me.
"Shit, just mad cause I can't find this bitch. I mean, damn
where the fuck could they be hiding," I fussed. I was ready
to get at them so that I could go on vacation. My baby had
been telling me that she wants to go to Jamaica for the past
month.
"I got niggas all overlooking for the ass. I know the nigga
get high because one of my lil niggas said that he copped
from him a while back. So, I got him on the lookout," Keys
added. That's why he was my nigga because he was always
on point. I was happy that he was now a part of the family.
"Good, I'm going to head home so that Kyndall can get
some rest. Just call me if you hear something."
"Will do," he said, dapping me up. I knew that he was
going to be on point, so I wasn't really worried.
It took me no time to get home. When I walked in the door,
it was smelling good as always. That was one of the things
that I loved about my baby; she made sure that she cooked
for a nigga every day. I can't remember the last time that I
had to eat fast food.
"What, you cooking baby?" I asked as I made my way into
the kitchen. She had both of the kids in the kitchen with
her. Cassidy was in the bouncer and CJ big ass was still in
his walker.
"Shrimp and chicken pasta. I'm tired so I wanted to cook
something quick." I just nodded and walked over to my
baby girl. She was chilling watching her mother. "Don't
forget that they have a doctor's appointment Friday baby."

My baby made sure that I knew everything that was going on with the kids. I looked down and CJ was making his way to me. I picked him up with my free hand and sat him on the counter. His fat ass just started laughing. I knew that he was going to be goofy as hell.

"Daddy babies miss him?" I asked as I kissed Cassidy's jaw. She just smiled like always. I was so happy that God blessed me and Kyndall with her. I knew that she deserved to have a baby, and I was happy that I was the one that was able to give it to her. It was crazy being with someone that you have been in love with since you were a kid. I knew that I loved Kyndall a long time ago. The one regret that I had was not pursuing her before Keem. I knew that I would have saved us both a lot of trouble. Hell, she wouldn't have gone through so much with Keem. I noticed that she was just staring at me.

"Yo, why you looking at me like that?" I asked as I watched her. She turned around because she hated for me to ask her that, but I didn't care. She was mine, and I could ask whatever I wanted. I just stood there looking at all that ass she had behind her. She has gotten so thick since she had the baby and I was loving every moment of it. She swore that she needed to lose weight.

"The food will be ready soon; go ahead and sit them down so that you can shower." I did as I was told. I knew that meant that I would be looking after them for the rest of the night. Me and my baby were a team. When she was tired, I watched and vice versa. I couldn't have asked for a better woman. She took CJ in with no question. I knew that shit would have never happened if it was Nadia.

Just as I was getting out the shower, Kyndall came and told me that it was time to eat. A nigga was hungry as hell. I had been out in the streets all damn day. It seemed that I had been sticking my hand in the street shit more than I had in the past. I guess it was more so because Luke was at home a lot. Shawnee's ass was needy. One day, we were at the warehouse counting, and her ass called I know at least twelve times. I just told his ass to leave.

I stood at the kitchen entrance looking at Kyndall tend to the kids. That shit had me smiling big as hell. I was going to marry her ass ASAP. There was no way that I was going to let her go. I took a seat next to her and dug into my food. The shit was so good that I finished in like five minutes and went to get more. I was about to dig back in and my phone rang. I saw that it was Keys, so I hurried and answered. It was late so I knew that he had some good news, otherwise he wouldn't have been calling me this late.

"Yo," I answered.

"Meet me at the warehouse," was all he said before hanging up. Kyndall gave me this look that I knew all too well. She was finna get on my ass. I just held my head down so that I could finish my food.

"Who the hell was that?" she questioned before I had the chance to stick the fork in my mouth.

"That was Keys, baby," I assured her. I didn't need her thinking that I was doing shit wrong.

"Oh," was all that she said. "I don't want you going to his house. I don't trust that hoe that he with. He needs to come here and see you," she said. I just laughed because I knew that she was dead ass.

"Ok baby. I need to run to the warehouse. It shouldn't take me long," She just nodded. I knew that she wanted to say more but she didn't, and I was thankful for that.

I jumped up soon as I was done eating and headed out the door. Luckily, I had on a Nike sweatsuit already. I slipped my Timbs on and headed out the door. It took me no time to make it to the warehouse. Luke was pulling up at the same time that I was. He looked like he was tired as hell.

"Damn nigga, you ok," I asked as we walked in the door.

"I'm good. I was sleep when this nigga called and so was Shawnee. You know how her ass is when she gets woken up. Hell, you been knowing her ass longer than me." His ass wasn't lying; she hated to be woken up out of her sleep. "I know she cursed yo ass out," I laughed. He just nodded. When we walked in, Keys had two people tied up. They had bags over their heads. I could tell that one was a female and one was a male by the shoes that they had on.

Keys pulled the bags from their heads and a big ass smile graced my face. He had come through and I was going to make sure that I paid him good for that. When he pulled the bags off, Nadia looked like she had seen a ghost. Keem, on the other hand, a blank look on his face. I knew that he would be that way. Hell, he looked like he was high as hell. "How the fuck did you find this duo," Luke asked as he took a pull from the blunt that he was smoking. That's all his ass did.

"So, this lil bitch I used to bust down called me mad because some nigga that she was fucking with was overstaying his welcome. Imagine my surprise when I got there and these two were laid out after what looked like a good fuck session," Keys explained. Keem always let pussy get him fucked off.

"So, Nadia. This nigga was more important than CJ?" I asked. I could tell that she was high, so she was gon' have a dumb ass answer.

"I told him that I would come back," she dumbly said. Nadia was a waste of beauty. She could have been a good woman to someone, but she decided that getting high was better. I remember when I met her, I thought that she would be my wife, hell. Now look at her; she was a strung-out hoe. I was ashamed to say that I had a baby with her.

"End this bitch." With that, Keys blew her head off. I knew that I could have done it but I didn't want to have to tell CJ that I was the one that killed his mother. I turned to Keem and he was still there looking zoned out. I was finna asked the nigga what was up, but Keys didn't give me a chance.

He sent a bullet through his head. Hell, I was surprised that he waited for us to get here.

"Feed that bitch to the fishes but let that nigga get found. I need to make sure that baby gets paid for her pain and suffering."

"Say no mo," he replied as I walked off. All I wanted to do now was go home and lay with my baby.

"That was fast," she said as I walked in the door. She was dressed in some boy shorts and a sports bra. My dick got hard soon as I laid eyes on her.

"Yea. I see you were ready for me to get home." I grabbed her ass as she walked to the stairs. She couldn't have thought that I was going to just let her have it all in my face and not touch.

"You so damn nasty," she cooed. I knew that she liked that shit. That's why she was wearing it.

I stood at our bedroom door watching her move around the room. I would have never thought that we would be together. This was more than I could ask for.

"So we found them," I blurted.

"Ok," was all that she said.

"That's all you gon' say?"

"Yep. What else is there for me to say. I know that meant that they are dead. I also know to act as if I'm shocked and surprised when I get the call about Keem," she added. I just looked. This girl was something else. She knew me too well. Now that that was out the way I was ready to slide inside of her. I needed my calm after the storm and Kyndall was just that.

Epilogue

Kyndall

One year later...

"Baby get CJ before his running ass falls," I fussed. We were in Jamaica finally. I had been asking to go for a long time and we were finally here. My baby had gone all out. We had a private island all to ourselves. The whole family was here. That was more than I could ask for. Keys and his hoe were even here.

After I got the call to identify Keem's body, life changed. Hell for a few days I was depressed. Not because I missed him but because I felt that it was my fault that he was dead. When I got that check in my hand all of that shit went away.

"Cassidy," I yelled. She was running near the water and that was scaring the hell out of me. I knew that Luke wasn't going to let anything happen, but I wasn't taking chances. Six months ago, I adopted CJ so now he was legally my baby. Also, Cash and I got married the same week. We didn't have a wedding. We just went to the courthouse. It was just the family. I didn't really need a big wedding because I had one with Keem.

"Don't be yelling at my baby," Cash said coming to her rescue as always. That little girl didn't do anything wrong in his eyes.

"Tee- Tee Kyn look," Joi yelled as she made her way to the water where her father was. Luke was in the water with him and Shawnee's son Lucas. He was the fastest damn baby. I thought that our kids were big, but he was bigger. I sat back and watched as they all played in the water. Cassidy had made her way down to the water as well.

"Girl what the hell, you doing all the way up here," Shawnee asked as she walked up.

"Nothing girl, just watching."

"Damn, my husband fine," she said as she took a seat next to me. Yes, you heard her right; her and Luke had been married for a while now. Hell, I guess that nigga said that he wasn't going to let her ass get away.

"Here come yo bestie," Shawnee jokes as Chrissy, Mom-Mom, and Keys walked up.

"Girl yes, Mom-Mom been my bestie for years," I said. I knew that she was talking about Chrissy, but she also knew not to play with me. I still didn't fuck with her. Hell, she didn't either. She didn't do any more than speak. Mom-Mom was cool with everyone, so she always talked to her. My mother-n-law talked to her as well but that was about it. I watched as she wobbled. Yeah y'all heard right wobbled, her and Keys were expecting a little girl. Keys was holding her hand like she was a baby. I guess he thought that she was going to fall. Keys was the only reason that I was cool with her being around, she made him happy and he had become like a brother so as long as he was happy so was I. Life for all of us was good. This was all that I could ask for. My family was complete.

The End...